Crazy for Cricket

DAVID WARNER

with J.V. MCGEE and J.S. BLACK,
Illustrated by JULES FABER

SIMON & SCHUSTER
AUSTRALIA
A CBS COMPANY

CRAZY FOR CRICKET – THE KABOOM KID BOOKS 1–4
First published in Australia in 2017 by
Simon & Schuster (Australia) Pty Limited
Suite 19A, Level 1, Building C, 450 Miller Street, Cammeray, NSW 2062

Containing:
The Big Switch
First published by Simon & Schuster Australia, 2014
© David Warner and J.V. McGee 2014

Playing Up
First published by Simon & Schuster Australia, 2014
© David Warner and J.S. Black 2014

Keep it Down!
First published by Simon & Schuster Australia, 2015
© David Warner and J.V. McGee 2015

Hit for Six
First published by Simon & Schuster Australia, 2015
© David Warner and J.S. Black 2015

10 9 8 7 6 5 4 3 2

A CBS Company
Sydney New York London Toronto New Delhi
Visit our website at www.simonandschuster.com.au

© David Warner, J.V. McGee, J.S. Black 2014, 2015, 2016

National Library of Australia Cataloguing-in-Publication entry
Creator: Warner, David Andrew, author.
Title: Crazy for Cricket: The Kaboom Kid books 1–4 / David Warner;
with J.V. McGee, with J.S. Black, writers; Jules Faber, illustrator.
ISBN: 9781925596496 (paperback)
Series: Kaboom Kid: 1–4.
Target Audience: For children.
Subjects: Warner, David Andrew.
Cricket—Australia—Juvenile fiction.
Cricket players—Australia—Juvenile fiction.
Cricket—Batting—Juvenile fiction.
Other Creators/Contributors:
McGee, J.V., author.
Black, J.S., author.
Faber, Jules, illustrator.

Cover design: Hannah Janzen
Cover and internal illustrations: Jules Faber
Typeset by Midland Typesetters, Australia
Printed and bound in Australia by Griffin Press

FSC
www.fsc.org
MIX
Paper from
responsible sources
FSC® C009448

The paper this book is printed on is certified
against the Forest Stewardship Council® Standards.
Griffin Press holds FSC chain of custody certification
SGS-COC-005085. FSC promotes environmentally
responsible, socially beneficial and economically
viable management of the world's forests.

CRAZY FOR CRICKET COLLECTION

The Big Switch

DAVID WARNER

with J. V. MCGEE, Illustrated by JULES FABER

SIMON & SCHUSTER
AUSTRALIA
A CBS COMPANY

FOR MUM & DAD

FORMULA 1 DNA

CONTENTS

CHAPTER 1

KABOOM TAKES A BOW

Davey Warner gripped his bat. Squinting in the sunlight, he watched as his arch-rival, Josh Jarrett, paced out his run-up at the far wicket. At last Josh turned and faced him. Even from this distance, Davey could see the determination in Josh's eyes as the star all-rounder gave the ball a final polish.

This was it. The last ball of the match, and Josh's team, Shimmer Bay, were ahead by five runs. Davey's team, the Sandhill Sluggers, had put up a fight, but they'd been the underdogs from the start. Now Shimmer Bay appeared certain to win the match and seize the number-one spot on the ladder.

Davey glanced around. Josh, who was Shimmer Bay's captain, had changed his field because Davey was a left-hander. Josh's team played like real professionals.

'Come on, Josh, bowl him a bouncer!' someone shouted from the sideline. The Shimmer Bay supporters were as determined as their players to see the Sluggers go down. They were always shouting out advice that even Josh Jarrett ignored, despite the fact everyone said he was cricket's most well-mannered, best-behaved all-round Mr Perfect.

Davey glanced over at the Sluggers'
supporters and players. Benny, their coach,
was present, but he was deep in conversation,
and Davey guessed he *wasn't* talking about
cricket. Davey's best mate, Sunil, gave him
a wave. There was his friend George, and
Kevin, who'd skipped Vietnamese school to
catch the game. Even his big brother, Steve,
had turned up.

'Go, Davey! You can do it!' Davey's mum
and dad were cheering from the sideline,
but they didn't sound confident. Why
would they? The Sluggers were as good as
finished.

Davey took his position at the crease.
Trying to focus his mind, he tapped his bat
on the ground. It was his special bat made
of English willow and signed by his heroes,
Ricky Ponting and Shane Warne. The bat was
called Kaboom, and it felt heavy and powerful

in his hands. He raised Kaboom to his lips and gave it a kiss for good luck. He was ready.

Josh began his run-up. He pounded towards the bowler's crease and let the ball fly. It was fast and short down the leg side.

Davey swung Kaboom and hit the ball clean and true. It soared into the sky and away, over the trees by the boundary. Six! *Six!*

Davey Warner had snatched the match from the jaws of defeat! The Sandhill Sluggers had won!

The Sluggers and their supporters cheered wildly. The Shimmer Bay supporters were already packing up.

Davey looked down at Kaboom. 'Thanks, mate,' he said to his special bat. 'I couldn't have done it without you.'

Kaboom nodded before leaping out of Davey's hands. The bat waddled out into the middle of the pitch . . . and took a bow . . .

Davey heard a squawk. The fielders had turned into seagulls and were flying off in every direction. Even Josh Jarrett had sprouted a pair of wings.

The other batter ran towards him. It was Max, his dog – and he was wearing a tutu in the Sluggers' colours of green and gold.

Max gave him a big wet kiss on the face. Ugh! Max smelt bad – he must have rolled in something.

Oh no! It's a dream! Davey woke with a start. Max was standing on top of him, licking his face. The dog stank like something dead.

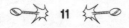

'Get off!' Davey shouted. He pushed Max onto the floor and squinted in the morning sunshine. He couldn't believe it. It had all seemed so real. Josh Jarrett, the Shimmer Bay supporters, Mum and Dad looking unsure . . . Kaboom taking a bow – and Max in a tutu. No, it definitely had been a dream.

And then reality hit, and Davey felt like pulling the blanket over his head and going back to sleep until the cricket season was over. Because the truth was, just three days earlier the Sandhill Sluggers had *lost* to Shimmer Bay. Davey hadn't hit a six – instead, all-round Mr Perfect Josh Jarrett had. And worse, Shimmer Bay were now top of the ladder, leaving the Sluggers stuck at equal second with the Crabby Creek Crickets.

It was too terrible to contemplate. Davey pulled the blanket over his head and tried to think about something else. Then he remembered it was the summer holidays and he and Sunil could meet up with the others for a game of cricket on the beach. Life wasn't so bad after all.

He threw the blanket off.

Davey's mum stuck her head around the door. 'Ah, you're awake. Better get up. Can't be late for your first day back at school!'

Davey pulled the blanket back up over his head and let out a groan.

'Good heavens!' he heard his mum exclaim. 'What have you been rolling in, you dreadful dog?'

Max barked. At least someone was happy the school year had started.

CHAPTER 2
MID-OFF MAX

Mrs Trundle, the school principal, had made it clear on countless occasions that Max was not to attend school under any circumstances whatsoever.

Unfortunately, Max had never paid any attention. So when Davey took off on his bike

in the direction of Sandhill Flats Primary, the dog was close behind, nipping the bike's back wheel and yapping loudly.

Davey found his friends already playing cricket at the bottom of C playground. No teacher was in sight, so Max was in the clear.

Sunil screwed up his face. 'What's that smell?! Warner! Have you been rolling in doggy doo again?' He laughed.

'Deep, you'll be in it in a minute,' Davey replied, pushing his friend so hard he almost fell into a puddle of what looked suspiciously like runny poo. 'It's Max,' he said.

Kevin McNab and George Pepi wandered over, holding their noses. 'Good to see you, Warner,' Kevin said in a nasally voice. He put his arm around Davey's shoulders. 'Come to learn how to play cricket, have you?'

'Very funny, McNab,' Davey said.

'I heard what happened against Shimmer Bay. You Sluggers obviously need help.'

'And you need a brain transplant.'

It wasn't exactly a killer line, but Kevin seemed to like it because he grinned. 'Oh well, give me a call if you need any tips. Maybe one day I'll join the team.'

Davey wished Kevin *would* join the Sluggers, but he couldn't because his mum made him go to Vietnamese school on Saturdays, which was when the Sluggers played.

'Come on, guys. It's nearly bell time!' Sunil called.

When everyone was in position, George bowled a leg break to Kevin, who lofted it

towards the mid-off fence. Max caught it on the full. Kevin was out.

'Stinking dog!' Kevin threw down his bat. 'You're in, Warner. But watch out for that dishlicker. He's getting good!'

Davey took Kaboom out of his backpack, then pulled out his special cricket cap and put it on his head. It was just a faded green trucker's hat, but Davey called it his 'baggy green' and had stuck a picture of the Australian cricket team's badge on the front.

'Okay, Deep, give me all you've got!' he shouted.

Sunil bowled a fast one outside Davey's off stump.

Davey drove it straight into Max's open jaws. Max smiled through his catch.

Davey was out for a duck. 'Max, you're a menace!'

Sunil guffawed. 'He's good is what he is. But, hey, can't get out first ball. Go again.'

Davey hated being given a second chance almost as much as he hated getting out. He faced up again.

Once more Max caught him out. The dog now had a hat-trick of catches.

'You'll have to do better than that if you want to beat Max the Axe,' Kevin called out.

Davey glared at his dog. 'Max the Muppet, more likely.'

Max grinned the way dogs do.

'Hey, Shorty! Out again? Maybe you should give up and play a *real* game.' Big Mo Clouter, the school's best footy player, had appeared out of nowhere and was standing menacingly beside the wicket while Sunil prepared to bowl.

Six years of putting up with Mo had taught Davey that the best thing to do was pretend the swaggering lump of wood was invisible.

Sunil did the same. 'One more chance!' he called to Davey before running in. But as he was about to bowl the ball, Mo stuck his foot out and tripped him.

It was a pathetic trick and Davey could hardly believe it had worked, but now Sunil was sprawled on the ground eating dirt.

Mo hooted then gagged. 'Aww, that dog's stinky! I gotta get out of here! Weird smells make me sick!' He ran off in the direction of the toilets.

Sunil got to his feet and dusted himself off. He turned to run in again.

'Warrr-*ner*!'

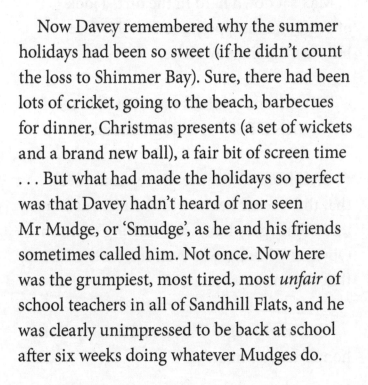

Now Davey remembered why the summer holidays had been so sweet (if he didn't count the loss to Shimmer Bay). Sure, there had been lots of cricket, going to the beach, barbecues for dinner, Christmas presents (a set of wickets and a brand new ball), a fair bit of screen time ... But what had made the holidays so perfect was that Davey hadn't heard of nor seen Mr Mudge, or 'Smudge', as he and his friends sometimes called him. Not once. Now here was the grumpiest, most tired, most *unfair* of school teachers in all of Sandhill Flats, and he was clearly unimpressed to be back at school after six weeks doing whatever Mudges do.

'Yes, Mr Mudge?'

'What is that dog doing at school? *AGAIN!* How many times have you been told?' Mr Mudge marched up to Max and grabbed him by the collar. 'Aargh! What's that smell?!'

Max sat down hard in the dirt, a look of profound disappointment on his face. He wasn't going anywhere.

'Get this malodorous mutt out of here THIS MINUTE!' Mr Mudge bawled.

Even from a distance, Davey could see that the teacher's ears, which stuck out from under lank grey hair, were turning crimson. Obviously Mudge was even sorrier than Davey that the holidays were over.

'Yes, Mr Mudge,' Davey said meekly. 'Max, home!' he commanded.

Max looked balefully at Davey and stayed put.

'Max, HOME! NOW!'

Max didn't move a whisker.

Davey trudged over, grabbed his dog by the collar and dragged him towards the school's side gate. 'Straight home,' he said into the animal's ear, before giving him a quick pat and pushing him through. 'No side trips.'

Max threw him a look that said *I can't promise anything* and slunk off.

When Davey returned to his friends, Mr Mudge was lecturing the boys on school rules about dogs and cricket.

'I'll be watching you lot,' he said. 'Do anything silly and I'll be putting an end to all

this cricket.' He looked at Davey. 'And get rid
of that hat! You're out of uniform!'

Finally Mr Mudge finished his tirade and
turned to leave.

'A few more balls, Deep,' Davey said quietly
to Sunil.

At that moment the bell rang.

'Put it away *immediately*!' Mr Mudge
bellowed as he stomped off.

The boys gathered their belongings and
trudged in the direction of the quadrangle.

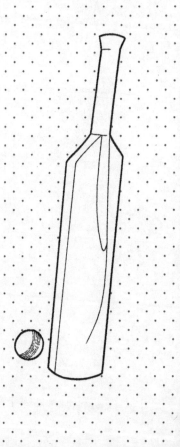

CHAPTER 3

MO'S MAMBO

'I need performers and volunteers to help with this year's Welcome to Kindy showcase. All you clever year sixes in particular – this is your chance to shine!' The smiling teacher addressing the assembly was new at the school.

She'll stop smiling pretty soon, once things settle down, thought Davey, who was sitting up the back with the rest of Year Six.

It was the first assembly of the year, and it seemed to be dragging on forever. There'd been announcements about no ball games in B playground and no running in A playground, and now the Welcome to Kindy showcase. No wonder everyone was whispering and fidgeting and scratching.

The new teacher pressed on. 'So come and talk to me about—'

Suddenly Mrs Trundle burst into rhythmic clapping. The whole school clapped back.

When everyone was quiet, Mrs Trundle seized the microphone. 'Thank you, Ms Maro,' she said, nodding in the direction of the now startled new teacher.

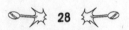

But Ms Maro wouldn't be silenced. 'Students, come and talk to me about your ideas for the showcase,' she shouted. 'Singing, dancing – anything you think the kindies and their parents will enjoy.' She looked across at Mrs Trundle and smiled. 'Thank you, Mrs Trundle. I've finished now.'

Mrs Trundle's eye twitched. She waved a wad of papers at the students. 'It's time to join your new classes,' she said in an imperious voice. 'Listen for your name, remember your teacher and, at the end of assembly, follow that teacher to your new classroom.'

Davey and his friends looked at each other. There were usually three Year Six classes, so chances were they'd be split up.

'We'll start with Year One,' Mrs Trundle said, looking across at Year Six with a smirk on her face.

Year Six groaned and zoned out.

Around four hours later, Davey came to.

'David Warner . . .' Mrs Trundle's voice was sounding tired. 'Sunil Deep . . .'

'Yes!' Davey whispered.

'Mo Clouter . . .'

Davey sucked in a breath.

'George Pepi . . .' Mrs Trundle's voice sounded husky. 'Bella Ferosi . . . and Kevin McNab.'

The boys punched the air. They were all in the same class. It was going to be one awesome year.

'Your class is 6M, and your teacher is . . .'

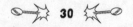

Davey and his friends stared at each other in horror. The M in 6M could stand for only one thing.

Mrs Trundle's voice was almost gone. '. . . Mr Mudge,' she wheezed.

'Warner, Deep, McNab and Pepi are to sit at different tables. There'll be no talking about cricket in my class!'

It was still morning on the first day of the school year and Mr Mudge's ears were already vermilion. 'Warner, you sit there.' Mudge pointed to the place between Bella Ferosi and Mo Clouter. 'Hopefully Bella and Mo can keep you on track.'

Bella, who was school captain and had never answered a question incorrectly since she was born, gave her neat brown ponytail a flick. She smiled kindly at Davey as he trudged towards her.

Davey pulled out his chair, set down his belongings and squeezed in next to Mo.

Mo made a face and grabbed Davey's ruler. 'I'll show you how to play cricket, Shorty,' he said, brandishing the ruler like a cutlass.

Davey smiled bitterly before looking around for his friends, now scattered to the far corners of the room. Sunil made a sympathetic face. There was nothing to be done, so Davey tried to tune in to the drone of Mr Mudge's voice.

'For my holiday, I went on a lawn bowls tour up the coast,' Mudge was saying. 'Every day we played in a new place against a new team. It was a dream come true!' He threw his arms wide in excitement.

Davey had never heard the old grump speak
with such passion.

'So now, I'd like *you* to write a short
recount about something you did during the
holidays.' Mudge smiled. 'There's just one
rule.' He raised his finger and pointed at
Davey, Sunil, George and Kevin in turn.
'No cricket. If I read anything about
cricket, you'll be picking up papers all
lunchtime.'

Back in third grade, Davey had worked out
that Mudge didn't like cricket much. Now it
struck him – Mudge *despised* cricket.

Davey looked at the blank piece of paper
in front of him. What else was there to write
about? Uncle Vernon's record-breaking burp
at Christmas lunch? The day Dad fell off
the veranda and landed on Mum's cactus?
Or when Sunil nearly choked on a Whopper

Chomp lolly, and Davey had to thrash him on the back to save him? All fun times, but not as much fun as playing cricket.

Suddenly he felt something sharp on his cheek. He looked up. Mo was laughing silently. A dozen or so paper spitballs were lined up on the desk in front of him. Wielding Davey's ruler like a tennis racquet, Mo was batting spitballs in his neighbour's direction.

Next Mo took aim at Bella. The school captain, who'd had her head down all the while, was studiously writing, her free hand covering her work so no one could copy.

Davey peeled the spitball off his cheek and tried to focus again on his story.

'*Ouch!*'

Davey looked up. Now Mo had his head down and was working quietly. The ruler lay by Davey's hand.

Bella picked a spitball off her face and raised her hand. 'Mr Mudge,' she said in a clear voice.

'Yes, Bella?'

'Davey Warner is hitting spitballs with his ruler. One got me in the face.'

Mo sniggered.

Mr Mudge's ears turned beetroot. 'Whhh–a–a–a–t? Warner, I'm giving you your first warning. One more and you're on lunchtime detention. Hand me that ruler. Now get back to work!'

Davey passed the ruler to Mudge. There was no point trying to clear his name. Instead, he tried to get on with his schoolwork.

But as he scribbled out the story of his dad's cactus accident, his mind returned to Mo's trick. He had to admit that Mo was on to something. He'd been hitting left and right, switching the ruler back and forth as if he was playing tennis.

Maybe, Davey thought, he could try a switch like that when he was batting. And maybe, then, he could beat Max at his own game . . .

CHAPTER 4
TRAINING TRY-OUT

'Out!' Sunil held up his index finger.

George punched the air. 'Mouldy Max strikes again!'

Max had caught Davey out at silly mid-off for the hundredth time that day.

Davey threw down Kaboom and ran at his dog, hooting. Max took off, tearing across Flatter Park towards the beach.

After a minute or so, Davey stopped, puffed. He looked back to where the Sluggers were still training. Benny, the coach, was lugging cricket gear across the park.

'Max!' Davey called. 'Back here now!' For once, Max obeyed and together they trotted back.

'Hey, guys! Sorry I'm late! Had to see a man about a dog.' Benny dumped the gear on the grass. He bent over to catch his breath, clutching his bulging tummy as if it might explode.

Benny was almost always late for training – and matches, too, sometimes. The team didn't mind. Someone would bring a ball, some bats, a set of wickets or two, and they'd just get on with it.

Now Benny straightened up. 'Gather round, guys,' he called. 'We need to debrief.'

When everyone was standing in a ragged circle, Benny launched into his 'pep' talk.

'It's a real shame we lost to Shimmer Bay,' he said. 'Fact is, they probably deserve to be top dogs. That Josh Jarrett, in particular, is real class.'

Davey and Sunil looked at each other and rolled their eyes. Josh Jarrett might be 'real class' but he was also a pain in the posterior.

'Anyway, no use crying over spilt milk. Next match is against Batfish Beach Bantams. They're not much chop, but it's going to be tough.'

Davey, George and Sunil tried not to laugh. Benny always feared the worst. Weirdly, the more pessimistic Benny was, the better the Sluggers played.

'And as for the game after next, against the Crabby Creek Crickets . . .' Benny shook his head. 'They're equal number two with us now and looking good, so I can't see how we'll win that one.' He smiled sadly. 'Never mind. You Sluggers keep plugging on. Who knows? A bit of luck might come our way . . .' He scratched his tummy and let out a loud burp. 'So, back to what you were doing, while I go and grab myself a snack from the shop. Been so busy today I didn't have a proper lunch.'

Davey knew that Benny was never busy. He ran the corner shop with his wife, Barb, but she seemed to do most of the work. Benny read the paper a lot and was always popping out.

As Benny turned to leave, he screwed up his nose. 'What's that smell?' he said.

Max barked and took off after a seagull.

The Sluggers went back to their positions. They didn't mind that Benny had nicked off. It meant they could play cricket without an adult telling them what to do.

Davey was fielding on the boundary. It gave him time to think. Mo Clouter's pesky face appeared in his mind's eye, and he recalled how the great lug had swung the ruler like a tennis racquet. Mo had called it cricket. *Yeah, sure.* But thinking on it some more, Davey wondered whether he could try it not only to outsmart Max the Mutt but to help defeat the Bantams on Saturday.

'You're in again, Warner!' Sunil was waving to him.

Davey collected Kaboom from the sideline and took his place at the crease. He glared at Max, who was still fielding at silly mid-off. The way things were going, soon Max would be playing for Australia and have his own baggy green.

'Watch this,' he growled at his dog.

George bowled a leg break. Davey turned quickly, swapped the position of his hands and tried to drive it right-handed past Ivy Mundine. He missed, and the ball flew through to Dylan, the keeper.

A few balls later, Davey tried the trick again. This time he got an edge to the ball, which almost went onto the wicket.

 44

Max barked as if to say, *Give up, boss.
You know it's useless.*

'Stop mucking about, Warner!' George
shouted from the other end of the pitch.
'Hit it!'

Davey considered his options. He could try
the trick one more time or forget it as a bad
idea. He decided to give it one more try.

George came in to bowl. Again it was a
leg break. Davey turned, swapped his hands
and bam! He hit the ball straight over the
boundary and into the swamp.

'That good enough for you?' he called to
George.

George nodded slowly, and gave the
thumbs-up. 'Not bad, Warner.' He pointed.
'You might want to get Max, though.'

Davey saw Max leap into the swamp and lope through the mucky water in search of the ball. The dog ducked and dived before dashing out and back across the park, trailing slime. At least he had the ball in his mouth.

'Now that dog is totally pongo!' Sunil said, as Max shook slime all over them.

Davey looked smug. 'Maybe, but he didn't catch me!'

'And he's given me an idea,' Sunil said, a malevolent grin on his face.

Davey raised an eyebrow. 'Yeah? What?'

Sunil tapped the side of his nose. 'You'll see.'

CHAPTER 5

TRICK OR TREAT

That night, Davey's mum made him wash Max. It was the last thing he felt like doing, but even he had to admit that it was either that or send Max to the dog pound.

Sunil and his little sister, Lata, who lived next door, came over to help. They held Max

by the collar while Davey ran the hose over him before squirting some doggy shampoo onto his back.

'Can I help?' Lata asked. She wasn't much taller than Max, but she managed to rub the shampoo into Max's fur and work up a lather. Now the dog looked like a walking bubble bath.

'It's a pity, really,' Sunil said, sucking noisily on a Whopper Chomp, his favourite lolly. 'Max has been an inspiration.' He pulled the lolly packet out of his pocket and offered it to Davey and Lata. 'Here, let's finish these.'

Davey took a lolly before Sunil could change his mind. 'What do you mean "an inspiration"?' he said.

'You'll find out,' Sunil said. 'It'll be brilliant. Mo's gonna flip.' He grabbed Lata by the hand. 'Come on, you. We've got work to do,' he said,

before heading down the side path. 'See you tomorrow.'

Davey shook his head. He guessed Sunil was off to play with his chemistry set. But why?

Davey turned on the tap again and began to hose Max, but the dog ran off. By the time Davey caught him and finished towelling him down, it was dark. Now Max smelt like a mix of Hubba Bubba and hospital.

Davey couldn't get to sleep that night. For one thing, Max was snoring on the floor. For another, the dog's unique odour filled the room. As Davey breathed it in, his thoughts turned to his tricky switch-hit idea. It wasn't an easy shot, but he'd managed to pull it off once at training.

Maybe, with lots of practice, he could do it whenever he wanted. It could become his secret weapon, something he could use not only to outsmart Max, but to help the Sluggers outdo the Batfish Beach Bantams and even the Crabby Creek Crickets. Maybe (and this was a BIG maybe), one day he could use his secret weapon to hit Josh Jarrett out of the park for real and help take down Shimmer Bay Juniors.

But to get it right, he'd have to practise it every morning, every lunchtime and every afternoon. There was no other way.

Just before he finally fell asleep, Davey remembered Sunil. *I wonder what he's up to? And what's that smell?*

Cricket before school now followed a pattern. Max would catch Davey, then George, then Kevin – and George would bowl Sunil.

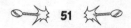

This time, when it was Davey's turn to bat, he decided to try his switch hit. He missed and nearly fell onto the stumps. The second time he tried it, Kevin almost caught him behind the wicket. The third time, it kind of worked, but the ball didn't go far. But the fourth time, it worked like a dream – and almost took out the eye of Mr Mudge, who had just appeared around the corner of the toilet block.

'Oh-oh,' George said. 'Smudge not happy.'

Spotting the approaching teacher, Max had the sense to make a beeline for the side gate. By the time Mr Mudge reached them, the dog was halfway home.

'Watch where you hit that ball or I'll be confiscating it.' Mr Mudge was out of breath and puffing like a steam train.

'And don't think I didn't see that dog, Warner,' he said. 'This is your last warning. If he's here again, you're going straight to Mrs Trundle.'

'Yes, Sir,' Davey said.

Sunil gulped, swallowing the lolly he'd been sucking. 'Mr Mudge?'

'Yes, Sunil?'

'Could I go into class early today? I want to practise my twelve times table.'

'Of course, Sunil,' Mr Mudge said, looking pleased. 'I wish some of these other ninnies,' he pointed at Davey, 'would spend more time on their schoolwork and less time playing cricket.'

Sunil smiled sweetly so his dimple showed. 'Thanks, Mr Mudge.' He picked up his bag and headed towards the classrooms. 'See you there,' he called.

When Davey and the others went into class, Sunil was already at his desk, his maths book open in front of him.

'How'd you go, Deep?' Davey said. 'Learn anything?'

'Twelve times twelve equals 147.' Sunil smiled and winked at his friends.

Mr Mudge appeared in the doorway. 'Ah, Sunil, how pleasing it is to see a student put in some effort. You won't regret it.'

'I find maths so much more interesting than cricket, Mr Mudge,' Sunil said.

'And it'll take you a lot further in life, young man.' Mr Mudge surveyed the room. 'Mr Deep here has been studying in his own time,' he said, 'setting an excellent example for the rest of you.'

'Sir?' Bella had her hand up. 'I study in my own time every morning before school, during lunch and after school. It's *one* reason why I mostly come first in things.' She gave her ponytail a flick.

'Thank you, Bella.' Mr Mudge's ears were candyfloss pink. 'You, too, set an excellent example for some of your less conscientious classmates.' He glared at George, then at Kevin, and then Davey.

His ears still rosy, Mr Mudge moved on. 'Speaking of setting an example, I want all the class to get involved in the Welcome to Kindy showcase. Ms Maro is open to any ideas.'

He made an odd face that Davey presumed was a smile. 'It's such a lovely way to introduce our newest pupils and their families to Sandhill Flats Primary. I'm sure some of you remember when you were in kindy and attended the showcase.'

'Arrgaaahhhggrrreeeeuuuwww!' The awful sound was loud in Davey's ear.

It was Mo. He appeared to be having some kind of fit. In front of him lay an open packet of Whopper Chomps.

Davey glanced back at Mr Mudge. The teacher's ears had turned carnation red.

'Clouter! Have you been eating lollies in class?'

Mo shook his head but was unable to speak. 'Arrgggrreeeuwwwahhhhh!' was all he could manage.

'What is the matter, young man?' Mr Mudge appeared perplexed.

Finally Mo got a word out. 'The smell! The smell!' He pointed to the bag of lollies. 'There – there's something in there!'

Davey became aware of a horrible stink. It was a bit like runny poached eggs and a bit like Max's farts after he stole the Christmas pudding.

Obviously Bella had caught a whiff of it too. 'It's disgusssting!' she screamed.

Davey glanced over at Sunil. His friend was engrossed in his times tables again.

'Get those lollies out of the room this minute!' Mudge's ears had turned violet. 'Clouter, you're on detention!'

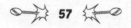

CHAPTER 6
SWITCH GLITCH

Mr Mudge soon deduced that while Mo Clouter may have been breaking class rules by trying to sneak a lolly, he wasn't responsible for the awful aroma emanating from the Whopper Chomp packet. Who *was* responsible, well, Mr Mudge couldn't be sure, because no one would confess to the crime.

Mo said he didn't know where the packet had come from. 'It was on my desk when I came in,' he whined. 'Whopper Chomps are my *favourite.*'

Davey tried to appear as confused as everyone else. But when Mr Mudge discovered that the Whopper Chomp packet contained a small open vial of rotten egg gas, Davey's suspicions were confirmed. Sunil's chemistry set was to blame. Mo must have come to the same conclusion, because he glared at Sunil with pure loathing.

Deeply unimpressed by the prank, Mr Mudge put the entire class on lunchtime detention for two weeks. 'Don't think you'll be sitting around, either,' Mudge barked. 'I have plenty of jobs for you.'

Everyone groaned, except Bella. Davey was particularly despondent. He needed those

lunchtimes to practise his new switch hit before
the weekend. Now he only had mornings and
afternoons to get it right.

At recess, Sunil tried to console him. 'At
least I didn't waste any Whopper Chomps on
Mo,' he said. 'Here.' He pulled a sweet from his
pocket and handed it to Davey. 'There's more
where that came from.'

The vampire teeth lolly was coated in sand
and fluff. Davey gave it a quick dust and
popped it in his mouth.

Sunil turned to his friends. 'You gotta admit
it was a good trick.'

Kevin and George nodded, impressed.
'How'd you do it?' Kevin asked.

'Iron filings and vinegar. Easy.'

Davey sucked thoughtfully on his Whopper Chomp. 'Deep, you're a master. Now we just have to work out how to get out of lunchtime detention.'

By the time the weekend came around, Davey and the rest of 6M had wasted hours of good cricket time picking up papers, sorting last year's lost property, and cleaning out Mrs Trundle's storeroom.

Davey had tried his best to practise his switch hit before and after school but, even though he was improving, he doubted it would be enough.

The match against the Batfish Beach Bantams was to be played at the Bantams' home ground, which gave them an edge, according to Benny. Still, the Sluggers had a few supporters, including Max, Davey's mum and dad, and Sunil's dad and his little sister, Lata, who was a fan and didn't like to miss a match.

When Sunil won the toss, he elected to bat first. 'Warner, Pepi, you're in,' he called. 'Now get out there and hit those Bantams for six.'

'Yeah!' Lata called from the sideline. 'Do it, Davey!'

Davey put on his helmet and adjusted his pads. With Kaboom in his hands, he felt ready for anything. There was no way the Bantams were going to outdo the Sluggers today, he decided.

After pulling on his gloves, he followed George onto the pitch, and took his position at the crease. When everyone was ready, the umpire gave the nod.

The first ball was a bouncer, and Davey let it go through to the keeper. He hadn't forgotten Benny's advice to take his time.

The second ball was wide.

It wasn't until the fifth ball that Davey swung Kaboom, but he only got an edge to it and was almost caught behind.

'Come on, Warner!' Sunil was shouting from the boundary line. 'Where's your secret weapon?'

Max barked. *Yeah, where is it, boss?* he seemed to say.

Davey wiggled his shoulders to relax, then took his position.

The bowler eyed him from the other end, before turning to go back to his mark. Then he ran in and let the ball fly.

 64

It was heading down the leg side. Now was his chance. He turned, switched hands and swung his bat. He felt the ball graze the edge.

'Howzat?' The Bantams were jumping up and down like battery bunnies.

Davey looked towards the bowler's end. The umpire raised his index finger in the air.

'Out!' he called.

'Out!' the bowler called.

'Ouch', you mean, Davey thought as he walked back to the boundary. Not only was he out, he was out for a duck.

After that, the Sluggers faltered then collapsed. George was caught at square leg for fifteen. Ivy started well and managed a four before being run out for eleven.

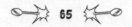

Then the middle order crumbled, and the Sluggers were all out for fifty-seven.

At morning tea, Benny was gloomy. 'They've done well,' he said, scratching his tummy anxiously. 'It's going to be tough from here on.' He looked at Davey. 'Remember what I said? No silly moves or tricky business. So what were you up to today?'

'Dunno,' Davey mumbled, giving the grass a good kick.

Sunil slapped him on the back. 'Don't worry, Warner. Leave it to us bowlers. We'll go in hard.'

Benny jingled his car keys in his pocket. 'I've got to nick off for a short while,' he said, surveying the circle of faces. 'No dreaming out on the field, okay? Everyone on the ball.'

Sunil hadn't been joking. He seemed determined to turn the match around, and had most of the team stand in close in an attacking field.

It worked, and the first Bantam was caught in slips for five runs. The other opener didn't last much longer, out for nine, caught at square leg by Ivy.

But following a middle-order slump, the Bantams' tail wagged, scoring plenty of quick runs to bring them almost level. With four balls to go, they were only three behind.

George bowled one down the leg side. The Bantam batter hooked it high.

'Mine!' Davey shouted, running to get under the ball. He caught it – but he fumbled and the ball tumbled to the ground.

'Aaaarggh!' The Bantams had scored two more. Now they needed just two runs off two balls to win.

George showed no sign of nerves as he prepared to bowl. His first delivery was a leg break. The batter tried to get to it, but misjudged the line and the ball went through to Dylan.

There was one ball to go. George bowled a flipper. This time the batter misjudged the length. The ball struck the wicket with a *thunk*, sending the bails flying.

'Out!'

The umpire raised his index finger.

Phew, Davey thought.

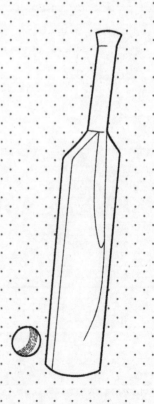

CHAPTER 7

PRACTICE IMPOSSIBLE

Before going to sleep that night, Davey had a chat with Ricky Ponting. He often talked to Ricky, whose face stared out from a dog-eared poster that was stuck to the wall behind his bed. Someone (Sunil) had climbed up and drawn a pointy beard on Ricky's chin and coloured in two teeth. But while the poster was fading, the Test cricketer's smile never did.

Davey was still smarting from his duck that morning, not to mention the dropped catch. If it hadn't been for George, who'd kept his cool under pressure, the Sluggers would have lost the match and possibly their equal second place on the ladder.

Now, as Davey lay in bed, he turned his head on a funny angle and looked up to Ricky for advice. *Should I give up on my secret weapon?* He stared hard at the face above him, so hard that his eyes began to water and he couldn't focus. Suddenly there was a flicker, and Davey could have sworn he saw his hero wink. Or was it a trick of the light?

''Night.' His mum was at the door. 'Someone wants to come in.'

Max leapt onto the bed and licked Davey all over his face. It was disgusting.

'Get off!' Davey gave the dog a push.

'Everyone drops catches occasionally,' his mum said, reading his mind. 'And even though it didn't work today, I reckon you'll get that switch hit thing working, with a bit more practice.'

She bent down and gave him a kiss that was much nicer than Max's.

'Now, I meant to tell you,' she said, ruffling his hair. 'I've volunteered for us to help out at Uncle Vernon's nursing home after school for the next week or so. We'll give all the old people a cup of tea and have a chat with them. Nothing too hard, and it makes such a difference to their day.'

'But—'

'You'll still have plenty of time to play cricket before school and at lunchtime, won't you?'

'Yeahhh,' Davey said, with his fingers crossed.

His mum gave him another kiss. 'So, off to sleep,' she said, switching off the bedside lamp. At the door she stopped. 'What does Ricky think about your secret weapon?'

'He reckons I should keep at it.'

'See?' she said. 'Practice makes perfect.'

Davey's secret weapon may have been looking pretty ordinary, but Sandhill Flats Primary had never looked so good. Thanks to the

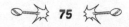

efforts of 6M while on lunchtime detention, the playground, storerooms, hall and library had all been tidied, cleaned, sorted and organised. Bella Ferosi had quickly taken charge, displaying quite a talent for giving orders.

Some students worked hard. Davey Warner, Sunil Deep, George Pepi and Kevin McNab were not among them. It was only when Mr Mudge asked for volunteers to weed and water the petunias outside Mrs Trundle's office that the boys showed any enthusiasm, hurriedly raising their hands. Given the job involved a hose, it might just be fun.

Mr Mudge narrowed his eyes. 'Can I trust you lot?' he said.

'Yes, Mr Mudge,' they replied in unison.

'Mmm. Mo, you can go too.' Mr Mudge looked at Bella. 'Ms Ferosi, you too. You're in charge. If any of these boys give you trouble, report them to me.'

'No problem, Mr Mudge.' Bella flicked her ponytail so hard it hit Davey in the eye.

Soon they were armed with gloves, garden forks and a bucket and heading for the petunia garden, Bella leading the way.

'Be careful to pull out only the weeds,' she instructed as she handed out the tools. 'The petunia plants have these big flowers on them and look like this.' She pointed. 'Now, let's get started.'

Davey reluctantly bent down and prised a weed out of the hard grey dirt. When he turned to throw it in the bucket, he saw that Bella was texting on her phone. 'Are you going to help?' he asked.

Bella gave her head a little shake, sending a shiver down her ponytail. 'I'm allergic to dirt,' she said.

Davey was already wishing he hadn't volunteered for this job. The weeding would take all lunchtime, leaving little time for the only fun bit – the watering. His friends looked as gloomy as he did.

Suddenly Mo began to work frantically. He gave Davey a push. 'Move over, Shorty. You're in my way,' he said. 'I'll get this job done in no time.'

The other boys stood back, amazed. Sure enough, Mo finished in minutes what would have taken them an hour.

'Very good, Mo,' Bella said. 'I'll tell Mr Mudge how you and I did most of the work.'

'Now the watering,' Mo said. He dusted off his hands and picked up the hose, which was connected to a tap around the corner. 'Here, Deep.' He handed the hose to Sunil. 'You hold this while I turn on the tap.'

Shrugging, Sunil took the hose. Never before had Mo been so diligent and helpful.

'Is it working?' Mo called from around the corner.

'No,' Sunil called back.

'What about now?' Mo had never sounded so friendly.

'Still not working.'

'Is it blocked?' Mo stuck his head around the corner. 'Maybe check the end.' His head disappeared.

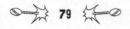

Sunil couldn't resist. He held the hose up to his eye and looked into the end. A huge spray of water hit him in the face.

'Clouter! You're toast!' Still clutching the gushing hose, Sunil vanished around the corner.

Davey heard the two boys shouting. Bella looked shocked. Seconds later, Mo and Sunil reappeared, both soaked.

'That's it!' Bella stamped her foot. 'Wait till Mr Mudge hears about this!' She stormed off in search of the teacher.

By the time Mr Mudge arrived, all five boys were dripping wet.

'My petunias!' Mrs Trundle had appeared in the doorway of her office. 'Mr Mudge, what on earth is going on?' Mrs Trundle sounded as if she thought Mr Mudge was to blame, and her eye was twitching.

Mr Mudge's ears glowed scarlet. 'Mrs Trundle, I must apologise. I'd hoped to surprise you. Instead, these boys have behaved disgracefully.'

Davey noticed that Mudge's ears had now turned indigo and he was shaking. He looked like he might self-destruct at any moment. 'You five are on morning detention as well,' Mudge said, grinning malevolently. 'There'll be no time for ball games. None at all.'

Davey's heart sank. Now his secret weapon was surely dead in the water.

CHAPTER 8

DETENTION CIRCUMVENTION

There was no way Max would be allowed to attend morning detention, so Davey locked the dog inside before grabbing his bag and helmet and pushing his bike down the side path.

As usual, he'd packed Kaboom, but now that he was on detention both morning *and*

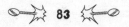

lunch, there'd be no time to play cricket and no time to practise his tricky switch hit at school. With only four days until the big game against the Crabby Creek Crickets, Davey had almost run out of time to get it right.

Out in the street, Sunil was loitering. He had one foot on his scooter but seemed reluctant to leave.

Davey climbed onto his bike, but he didn't feel like going either. 'I can't believe we have to spend every *morning* before school doing more stupid jobs with Smudge,' he groaned. 'And now Mum's got me sitting around with all the old fogeys at Uncle Vernon's every afternoon. 'When do we get to play cricket? It's so unfair!'

Sunil was usually the man with the plan, but today he seemed defeated. 'Yeah, it sure does suck,' he grumbled. 'And then to have to spend all day and all lunchtime with Smudge. It's intolerable!'

Sunil never used words like 'intolerable'. He was clearly upset.

'It'll be worse than *intolerable* if we're late,' Davey said. 'We'd better go.'

When the boys reported to the quadrangle for morning detention, Kevin and George were already there. Mo was there too, kicking a football *at* them rather than *to* them. Mr Mudge, however, was nowhere to be seen.

Then the new teacher, Ms Maro, appeared around the corner. She was leading a group of Year Sixes from another class.

'Ah, here they are,' she said kindly. 'Mr Mudge is training the new lawn bowls team this morning, so I offered to keep an eye on you.' She smiled and Davey noticed what nice brown eyes she had. 'Now, why don't you boys give us a hand? We're getting ready for the Welcome to Kindy showcase. There's lots to do!'

'Yes, Miss,' they mumbled. Helping Ms Maro had to be better than polishing the lawn bowls set, which is what Mudge had threatened to make them do.

'Follow me!' the teacher exclaimed, as if they were about to embark on an Easter egg hunt in a magical forest. She led them to A playground, where a group of gymnasts wearing what looked like bandicoot ears were practising on a vaulting horse.

The school choir was also gathered and already halfway through the school song.

Lead soprano Bella Ferosi was front and centre.

Still another group of students were on the grass, painting signs that said things such as 'Kanga's Kakestall' and 'Possum's Potions'.

'Possum's Potions?' Davey whispered to his friends. They all looked at each other and shrugged.

Ms Maro thought for a moment. 'Now, boys, perhaps you'd like to stand at the back of the choir,' she said brightly. 'I'm sure you know the school song. If you're not confident to sing along, just mouth the words. You know, like they do in music videos.'

Mo grumbled but did what he was told, pushing his way past Bella and into the choir's back row.

Sunil looked at Davey, then George and Kevin. 'Actually, Miss, I've been meaning to talk to you.' He smiled so his dimple showed. 'We're in the school cricket team.' He nodded in the direction of his friends. 'And I thought we could give the kindy kids and their parents a demonstration. Get the kids interested in sport early, you know? Develop some new talent.'

Ms Maro looked at Sunil as if he were her long-lost son. 'That's a wonderful idea!' she said. 'Do you think the other team members might also join in? It'd be great to have you all there showcasing your skills!'

'I'm the captain, so I should be able to make it happen,' Sunil said in an authoritative voice. 'But if it's okay with you, we'll start practising now. Tomorrow I'll make sure the whole team's here. We've got our own gear with us, see?' He held up his cricket ball with one hand

and pointed to Kaboom, which was sticking out of Davey's bag, with the other.

'Excellent, Sunil. Mr Mudge will be thrilled to hear that you boys have offered to participate!'

Ms Maro really did have nice eyes, Davey noticed. Her smile was lovely too.

'It's probably safer if we take it down to B playground,' Sunil said helpfully.

'Certainly,' Ms Maro said. 'Off you go!'

Davey had to hand it to his friend – he *was* a genius!

The boys set off, trying not to cheer until they were well out of earshot.

'Boys!' Ms Maro was beckoning them back.

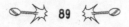

'I forgot to mention,' she said, when they stood before her once more. 'The theme for Welcome to Kindy this year is "Australian Animals".' She drew quotation marks in the air. 'So everyone will be dressed as marsupials.'

Ms Maro beamed as if she'd never heard of anything more fun. 'Why don't you dress up as kangaroos? The kindy kids will love it!'

'But where would we get the costumes from, Ms Maro?' There was an odd quaver in Sunil's voice that Davey rarely heard.

'You can help make them! All you need are ears and tails. We'll do the makeup on the day.'

'PPPPFFFfffffffffff! Ha-ha!' Mo Clouter, who had been standing in the back row of the choir scowling, was grinning like a demented pufferfish.

Ms Maro flashed Mo a warm smile. 'I know! It's going to be so much fun! Wait till you singers get *your* costumes!'

Mo's grin became a grimace.

CHAPTER 9
SECRET WEAPONS

With Ms Maro's blessing, Davey Warner and his friends managed to play some cricket during Monday's morning detention.

Sunil even convinced Ms Maro to speak to Mr Mudge about allowing them to practise for the Welcome to Kindy showcase during

lunchtime detention. The boys didn't expect the new teacher to have any luck on that score, but when she visited the cricketers on Tuesday morning, she informed them that Mr Mudge had agreed.

'I wonder what she said to convince Smudge,' Davey whispered, as Ms Maro headed back to the relative safety of A playground.

'I dunno,' Sunil replied. 'But I'm starting to think she's tougher than she looks. Remember how she stood up to Mrs Trundle in assembly? I reckon she has some kind of secret weapon of her own.'

'She must have. She's got us dressing up as kangaroos ...'

Detention was suddenly a whole lot more fun. With the whole team playing, it felt almost like a real match. Sunil, being captain, even went so far as to give Davey extra time at the crease, pounding him down the leg side so he could practise his switch hit, and letting him stay in even when he got out.

When the rest of the team complained about Davey getting all the batting time, Sunil bought them off with Whopper Chomps that he'd obtained on credit from Benny's shop.

It was an act of extreme generosity. 'Don't worry, Warner,' Sunil said when Davey fell over in shock. 'You'll have to pay Benny back – with interest. But first things first. You've gotta get this switch hit right before Saturday.'

Even Mr Mudge had a spring in his step. Like the cricketers, his new lawn bowls team were practising hard for the Welcome to Kindy showcase and were apparently showing great promise. Mr Mudge seemed more willing to overlook the minor misdemeanours of certain members of 6M. He even let slip that he'd agreed to dress up as a marsupial for the kindy welcome.

Only Mo, having been dragooned into the choir, seemed unhappy with the new arrangements. He was constantly whispering insults at Davey, and tried more than once to get him in trouble. But Davey didn't care. He wasn't the one having to practise lip syncing in the choir every morning.

By training on Tuesday evening, Davey's secret weapon was starting to come together. He was finding that he was better able to judge which balls to use it on, and his timing was improving, too. But when Benny finally arrived and gathered the team around him for his pre-training pep talk, he was decidedly unenthusiastic.

'We were lucky on Saturday and we probably didn't deserve it. And while I don't want to point the finger'—he pointed at Davey—'if we'd all taken our time and not tried anything clever, we could have done a lot better.' He looked Davey in the eye. 'You've got real talent, my friend. Don't waste it by taking silly risks. Ditch the switch, okay?'

Davey looked around at Sunil and George. Sunil's face showed no emotion, but he gave Davey a half-wink. George scratched his nose, but Davey noticed his friend had his fingers crossed.

'Now, I need to pop away for a short while to see—'

'—a man about a dog,' the Sluggers said as one.

Benny looked taken aback. 'Yeah, that's right. So get to it. I'll be back to pick up the gear.' He glanced again at Davey. 'Remember what I said . . .'

Davey nodded, but he'd already made up his mind. Ricky said he should go for it. His mum said he should go for it. Even his big brother, Steve, who never showed any interest in the Sluggers' fortunes, had said at breakfast that it could work. And, most importantly, *Davey* wanted to give it his best shot.

As soon as Benny's car turned the corner, the boys went back to their game. Sunil was in, but when Max caught him out (again), they started at the top of the batting order. Now Davey and George were in.

Dylan, their wicketkeeper, had a turn at bowling spin.

'Give Warner some down the leg side. And see if you can trick him with a googly,' Sunil called out.

Dylan bowled a few topspinners before surprising Davey with a flipper. Then he sent one down the leg side. Davey picked it, made the switch, hit it high and ran for three.

When he was back at the striker's end, Davey tried his switch again. It worked like a dream, and he slammed it high for four.

'You're getting better and better, Warner!' George called out.

'Yeah, good one!' Sunil called, running over. 'A bit more practice and it'll be a sure-fire scare-'em-off-the-pitch secret weapon.' He slapped Davey on the back. 'Along with my secret weapon, those Crickets won't have a hope!'

'Your secret weapon?' Davey frowned. 'Don't you go breaking any rules, Deep. We don't want to be disqualified.'

Sunil's expression was stern. 'I'd never do anything on the field that wasn't within the laws of cricket,' he said in his captain's voice.

At that moment, Ivy lobbed the ball in their direction. Davey caught it. 'Here. Stick to this secret weapon,' he said, handing the ball to Sunil. 'Now, give me one down the leg side.' He went back to his place at the crease.

Sunil bowled a bouncer. This time Davey's switch hit was perfect, and the ball went flying into the swamp.

'Six!' George shouted.

Max took off at a gallop. Moments later, he dropped the ball at Davey's feet.

'Thanks, boy,' Davey said, giving the dripping dog a pat. 'Aww, Max, now you stink again!'

CHAPTER 10
COSTUME CRICKET

By morning detention on Thursday, the
school cricket team's demonstration routine
for the Welcome to Kindy showcase was
coming together. Davey's switch hit was
looking even better. In fact, the team were
having so much fun they didn't want detention
to end.

When Davey and his friends did make it to class, Mr Mudge was so preoccupied with his lawn bowls team he not only failed to notice they were late, but forgot to mark their homework. It was a bonus for Davey and Sunil, who'd forgotten to do it.

When at last it was lunchtime, they were all itching to get to detention. On their way to C playground, they spotted the school choir practising.

Mo Clouter could be seen but not heard, standing in the back row glaring.

Sunil give him a friendly wave.

Mo's face turned purple.

Ms Maro, who was sitting with a group of kids on mats working with scissors and glue, called the cricketers over. 'Tomorrow morning we make the costumes, guys!' she cried, as though they'd just won a prize in a lucky dip. 'So come here as soon as you get to school. Then we've got the dress rehearsal at lunchtime.' Her brown eyes widened. 'I can't wait to see you all dressed up!'

'Ha ha!' Mo's face was wearing that awful pufferfish grin again.

Ms Maro nodded encouragingly at Mo.

'Can't you get us out of wearing ears and tails?' Davey hissed to Sunil once they were out of earshot. It was the only thing taking the shine off proceedings.

'I'm working on it. Maybe . . .'

Davey rounded the toilet block and spotted Max sitting patiently under a tree, waiting for the game to start.

'Oh-oh. Where's Smudge?' Davey said.

'With the lawn bowls team in B playground,' Kevin said. 'He'll be busy all lunchtime.'

'Good. Let's get started.'

When it was Davey's turn to bat, Max took up his position at silly mid-off and barked impatiently.

Kevin bowled a topspinner. Max stood ready to catch him again, but Davey switched sides and hit the ball to the boundary.

'Tricked you, brainless bow-wow!'

Max gave him the evil eye and trotted over to silly mid-on. He barked again.

Davey called out to Kevin. 'Give me another one like that!'

Kevin mixed it up, bowling a flipper.

Davey switched and slammed it high over Max's head.

'Max, you might as well go home,' Davey said. 'You're outclassed.'

Max sat on his haunches. *I'm not going anywhere*, he seemed to say. But when the bell rang, he made a dash for the gate and freedom.

Davey and his friends would have preferred to spend their second-last detention playing cricket, but as it turned out, making koala and kangaroo ears and tails wasn't as tedious as they'd expected.

The boys had to admit that Ms Maro's enthusiasm was contagious. She was so excited by all the fun to be had that soon they were laughing and joking as they glued pieces of fake fur onto cardboard and sewed long strips to elastic. It was certainly better than writing lines or picking up papers with Mr Mudge.

But dressing up in ears and tails was another matter, and when it was time for lunchtime detention on Friday they dawdled to A playground, where the dress rehearsal was to take place.

When they arrived, the school choir, now dressed as echidnas, were setting up. Mo looked like he'd eaten a bad prawn as he clambered into the back row.

Sunil and Davey gave him a friendly wave.

While the choir sang, the cricket team put on their costumes.

'You look like a meerkat,' Davey said to Sunil.

'And you look like an orangutan,' Sunil replied.

When the singing was over, Ms Maro clapped loudly. 'Beautiful!' she cried.

Next up were the bandicoot-eared gymnasts, who leapt and dived over the vaulting horse while the lawn bowls team, wearing platypus tails, set up. Directing proceedings were Mr Mudge and Mrs Trundle, but Davey was disappointed to see that neither teacher wore a tail.

The cricket team set up their wickets while the lawn bowlers ran through their routine. To Davey, lawn bowls seemed slow, even dull, but Mr Mudge and Mrs Trundle appeared to adore it, cheering and clapping and ooing and ahing. Davey couldn't understand it.

'Okay, guys, hit it!' Ms Maro shouted when at last it was the cricket team's turn.

Five minutes later, the cricket display was over and Ms Maro was brimming with admiration. 'You'll be playing for Australia one day!' she exclaimed, as everyone gathered around.

Sunil smiled so his dimple showed. 'Thanks, Ms Maro. But we'd play much better without the tails and ears. I'm worried we'll trip over or something.'

Davey, who was standing at Sunil's side, nodded. 'It could be dangerous, Miss,' he said.

'Yeah, it could be,' someone said in his ear.

Davey turned. Mo Clouter was standing right behind them. He had a look of concern on his face – for Ms Maro's benefit, Davey presumed.

 111

Ms Maro was thoughtful for a moment. 'Mmm. We better trim a few centimetres off those tails, then.' She put her hand into her pocket and pulled out a hairpin. 'And we'll use these to make sure your headbands don't slip.'

As one, the cricket team sucked in a breath.

'Davey Warner, there's a packet of hairpins in my desk drawer. Run and get them while we start on the tails.'

Ms Maro looked so pleased with her solution to the problem that Davey didn't have the heart to argue. So he set off in the direction of the teacher's room. But after just one step he toppled like a skittle and landed heavily on the grass with Sunil on top of him.

Davey felt an excruciating pain in his right ankle. 'Owww! What did you do, Deep? Get off!' He gave his friend a push.

'I didn't do anything!' Sunil tried to scramble to his feet, but fell over again.

Davey glanced down. His kangaroo tail was tied in a neat bow with Sunil's.

Ms Maro had a quizzical look on her face. 'Are you boys all right?' she said.

Sunil sat up and untied the tails. Then he got to his feet and tried to pull Davey up.

'Owwww!' Davey yelled again. When he did manage to get back on his feet, he found he could only stand on his left leg. And where his right ankle had once been there was a red lump the size of a cricket ball bulging out of his grey sock.

'PPPppffffffff!' Mo Clouter could no longer contain his amusement.

CHAPTER 11
MATCH UNFIT

Saturday dawned clear, sunny and still –
perfect weather for the big match between
the Sandhill Sluggers and the Crabby Creek
Crickets. Davey Warner's eyes snapped open
and locked with Ricky Ponting's. *Good luck,
mate*, Ricky seemed to say. *You can do it.*

Out in the kitchen, Davey's dad had rustled
up scrambled eggs and toast with fresh orange
juice. While Davey gobbled up his breakfast,
his mum packed Kaboom, his helmet, his
lucky waterbottle and some green zinc cream
in a backpack and left it by the door.

'Ready?' she asked, as Davey shovelled the
last forkful of egg into his mouth.

Davey nodded.

'Here you go, then.' She handed him his
crutches.

Davey stood slowly and balanced on his
right foot. Once he had a crutch under each
arm, he made his way out to the car. Even
though the match was on at Flatter Park, a
few minutes' walk away, Davey would need
a ride.

Sunil was waiting by the car door. 'Thought I might as well get a lift,' he said. 'Dad's bringing Lata down later.' He looked Davey up and down. 'You sure you need crutches? Maybe that doctor's wrong.'

'Mum's insisting.' Davey tried putting weight on his right foot. 'Owww! I can still bat, but you'll have to run for me.'

Sunil helped him into the car. 'Reckon you can still do your secret weapon?' He looked worried.

'Dunno,' Davey said, as Sunil loaded the crutches in through the car door. 'I need to be able to move my feet fast for that.'

When Benny saw Davey shambling across Flatter Park, he grimaced. 'Gosh, mate, that looks nasty. Guess you'll have to sit this match out, eh?'

Davey shook his head. 'Nup, I'm fine to bat. Just need Sunil to run for me.'

'You sure?' Benny looked from Davey to Sunil, clearly pessimistic.

'Fine by me,' Sunil said. 'Warner's going to be hitting all sixes and fours, so I won't have much to do.' He slapped Davey on the back so hard he almost fell off his crutches.

Benny narrowed his eyes. 'Well, no funny stuff, Davey.'

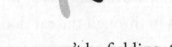

'Yes, boss.'

'I'm thinking you won't be fielding, though, eh?'

Davey shook his head.

'Well, we've got no twelfth man today, so

we'll be one down out there.' Benny sighed. 'Looks like those Crickets'll be singing.'

'Don't worry, Warner,' Sunil said when Benny had left, off to grab a sandwich from his shop across the road. 'You've got your secret weapon, and I've got mine. Between us, we can *squash* these Crickets.'

Davey frowned. 'Deep, don't you put us in it.'

Sunil smiled. 'Just something to keep it interesting.' He looked towards the road. 'Ah, here she is now.'

'Who?'

'Lata. She's doing a little job for me.'

'Lata? She's four!'

'Exactly. No one will suspect her.'

Davey shook his head. Sometimes it was better not to know. Sunil was clever, that's for sure, but his schemes didn't always pan out. Davey was about to say so when the umpire called the Sluggers' captain away for the toss of the coin.

The Crickets won the toss and elected to bat, so the Sluggers made their way out onto the field. Only Davey stayed behind, sitting by himself under a tree in a fold-up chair with his crutches beside him, stripes of green zinc cream on his nose.

The match started slowly. George was bowling, but the Crickets weren't taking any chances, hitting ones and twos and offering up no catches.

Davey watched, his fingers and toes crossed that a batter would get bored and do something risky. He glanced over at Lata.

She was a short distance away, watching the game with Sunil's dad and all the other Sluggers' supporters. When she saw Davey look over, she gave him a big wave.

'Hi!' Davey called. He'd need to keep an eye on her, he decided.

Then he noticed that one of the Crickets' supporters, who were sitting under trees further off, was waving in his direction, shouting. 'Hey, Shorty!' It was Mo with that pufferfish grin.

What's he doing here? Davey wondered. Mo hated cricket.

Out on the field, the Crickets were warming up and off to a solid start.

Davey glanced over at Lata again. Now she was near the Crickets' camp, throwing a stick for Max. She saw Davey look over and waved

again. She held up the packet of what looked like TizzyFizz sherbet. 'Yum!'

Davey gave her the thumbs up.

'Out!'

Sunil had clean-bowled one of the Crickets' opening batters for thirteen runs. Davey and the Sluggers' supporters clapped. Lata cheered.

'Boo!' It was Mo.

The Crickets' number-three batter made his way out to the pitch. Davey glanced over at Lata. Now she'd found a tennis ball and was throwing it to Max, who was catching it on the full. It looked harmless enough.

Sunil quickly took another wicket. Two overs later he trapped the Crickets' number four LBW with an inswinger.

Suddenly there was a bark. Max was chasing Lata's tennis ball across the field. Then he spotted some seagulls and tore off after them. The birds rose as one. Max began dashing around in circles, snapping at the air.

'Max! Get back here!' Davey shouted, grabbing his crutches and scrambling to his feet.

Max ignored him.

Davey didn't go after him – he knew it would be pointless trying to round up the dog on crutches.

The umpire called a halt to proceedings while supporters from both sides tried to herd the dog back to the boundary. But Max was having none of it, and it took them ten minutes to catch him and tether him to the fence so the match could continue.

Davey sat down again. *Was that Deep's secret weapon?* he wondered. If it was, it didn't work. In fact, the disturbance seemed to focus the Crickets. As if they suddenly had Sunil's number, they began hitting him around the park. Several fours and a couple of sixes later, they'd lost no more wickets and were racking up runs fast.

Even when George took over the bowling, the Crickets kept up the pressure. By morning tea and the end of the innings, they'd lost no more wickets and had scored ninety-two runs. It was a strong effort and Davey knew it'd be hard to beat.

The Sluggers looked red-faced and disappointed as they came off the field.

Back from the shop, Benny was handing out the water bottles. 'Not a bad effort, guys,' he said, 'but there's no doubt those Crickets are

on top.' He offered around the cut-up oranges.
'You've got an uphill battle. With Davey
here on crutches, I'd say it's looking almost
impossible.'

Sunil let out a groan.

'I know how you feel, mate,' Benny said.

Sunil growled and shook his head.

Davey had never seen his friend so
miserable after an innings.

'Yeah, it's terrible,' Benny moaned, nodding.

'*Lata!* What have you *done*?' Sunil threw his
piece of orange in the dirt and took off after
his little sister.

Thinking it was a game, Lata ran away,
giggling. Her dad watched, bemused.

Davey glanced at his teammates. Every single Slugger had a look of disgust on their face.

'Eeewww!' they yelled.

Now George threw his piece of orange in the dirt. 'These oranges are revolting!'

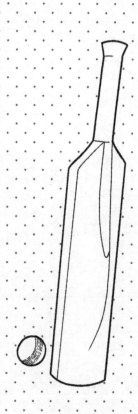

CHAPTER 12

BATTING FROM BEHIND

The Sluggers' oranges tasted so disgusting they had to be thrown in the bin.

'Any chance you could bring some over from the shop?' Davey's mum asked Benny.

Benny shook his head. 'None there. Barb threw them out yesterday. They'd gone all green and powdery.'

In the end, the Crickets gave the Sluggers their leftovers, but there wasn't enough to go round and most Sluggers went without.

Around the other side of the field, Sunil was speaking sternly to his little sister. No one could hear what he was saying, but when he'd finished, Lata marched back to her father with a furious frown on her face. Sunil looked just as irate as he returned to the sideline to pad up.

'What was all that about?' Davey asked his friend as they pulled on their helmets.

'Tell you later,' Sunil mumbled. 'Suffice to say my secret weapon's no longer operational. We're counting on yours now, Warner.'

Davey grimaced inside his helmet. Now he had a sprained ankle, he doubted whether he'd be able to pull off his switch hit. It took some fancy footwork, but he could barely stand on two feet, let alone make them dance.

When the batters and the runner were ready, they made their way out to the wicket, Sunil and George half-carrying Davey as he hopped across the grass. 'Owww!' he yelped more than once.

In contrast to the hot, tired and hungry Sluggers, the Crickets looked fresh-faced as they took their positions. Calum, their captain, set a tight attacking field, so much so the umpire had to order some of his players to take a step back from the pitch.

Davey and Sunil stood at the bowler's end and waited. George took his position at the crease.

The Sluggers got off to a slow start, thanks to a strong opening spell from one of the Crickets' best bowlers. Her first ball was wide, but from then on her line was good and the length varied enough to keep George on his toes.

George let the first few go through. It wasn't until the last ball of the over that he pulled off a glance past fine leg. He and Sunil ran for three.

During the next two overs, George played well, taking his time but making the most of any opportunities. Then, after George made a graceful sweep to square leg, Davey found himself at the crease.

Davey's plan was to take his time and try to play as much as possible off his good back foot. He left as many balls as he played, blocking singles when the ball was full, before playing a pull and hook through the leg side. He'd decided to use his switch hit only as a last resort because the footwork was so tricky, especially with a cricket ball for an ankle.

But the Crickets were on to him, and soon the bowler was sending down full-length balls to try to tempt Davey onto his injured front foot. Davey resisted the bait, sticking with his defensive shots and the odd back-foot drive when he could. But his aching ankle told him that his secret weapon, which depended on turning on his front foot, was probably a no-go.

In the fifteenth over, the Sluggers suffered a hammer blow when George tried a cut shot and was caught behind for thirty-one. Davey watched as his friend trudged back to the bench. The Sluggers were now on fifty-two. They'd need to pick up their run rate to get close to the Crickets.

Number three in the Sluggers' order was Ivy. As soon as she came to the crease, she was looking good. Davey watched as she hit a four off her second ball, before driving to deep extra cover for three more.

As Davey waited for the next ball, he looked across at Sunil.

'You okay?' his friend asked.

'Yeah, but I can't move my right foot so well.'

The bowler delivered an inswinger. Davey drove it to long-on. Sunil and Ivy ran, and ran again. The long-on fielder fumbled the ball, so they tried for another run. Suddenly the ball was in the hands of the bowler, who threw it at the wicket. As Sunil dived into the crease, the bails flew.

The Crickets leapt into the air. 'Out!'

Sunil clambered to his feet but stood his ground. Davey looked at the umpire, his heart in his mouth.

The umpire didn't move.

'That was out!' someone yelled from the sideline. It was Mo. He was still standing with the Crickets' supporters, waving his arms like an unhinged octopus.

The umpire still didn't move. 'Not out,' he said finally.

The Crickets shook their heads and went back to their positions. But even from the other end, Davey could see that his friend *had* made it in time.

As Sunil took up his position as runner at the bowler's end, he turned and gave Mo a friendly wave.

'Go the Crickets!' Mo hollered. Davey could see that even the Crickets' supporters were looking sideways at the bellowing turnip.

But while Davey had lived to see another over, Ivy was out LBW two overs later. After that, the Sluggers' middle order wavered, losing their next six wickets for just eighteen runs.

At eight wickets down for eighty-three, Sunil was batting next, so George came back out to run for Davey.

As the Sluggers' captain made his way to the striker's end, Davey took a deep breath. If he didn't pick up the pace, victory would soon be out of the Sluggers' reach and they'd lose their number-two position on the ladder. Davey knew he probably shouldn't have cared too much, but he did – a lot.

CHAPTER 13

SWITCH OR NIX

The Crickets' best paceman let the ball
fly. The ball looked straight and Sunil
played at it. But at the last moment it
swung out, glancing off the bat's edge and
sailing straight into the keeper's waiting
hands.

Sunil was out – for a golden duck. Shaking his head, his face set in a grimace, he walked.

The umpire raised his arm and the Crickets and their supporters cheered.

'YEAH!' someone thundered. It was Mo.

Davey watched as Joe, the Sluggers' last batter, trudged across the field to the striker's crease. With only two overs to go, the Sluggers needed ten runs to win. That meant at least five runs each over, which was much more than their current run rate.

Two balls went through before Joe played a late cut to backward point for one. Now Davey was at the crease, and the Crickets quickly changed their field for the left-hander.

Again the bowler tried to draw Davey onto his front foot, forcing him to let the ball go

through to the keeper. On the last ball of
the over, he managed to pull off a back-foot
cover drive. George and Joe ran a single. The
fielder fumbled the ball, so they ran again and
managed to turn the single into a three.

With one over left, the Sluggers were now
five behind and Davey was at the striker's
end again.

But halfway through the final over,
Kaboom hadn't even smelt leather let alone
struck it. When the fourth ball came down the
leg side, Davey decided it was now or never,
and turned, swapped his hands and made to
drive it up and over. Instead, the ball nicked
the edge and was just short of being caught
in slips.

There were two balls to go and the Sluggers
were still five runs behind.

'CRACK 'EM, YOU CRABBY CREEK CRICKETS!' Mo's face looked like it might pop at any moment.

Davey breathed in, wiggled his shoulders and took his position again. 'Come on, we can do it,' he whispered, tapping Kaboom on the pitch in front of him. But he had to let the bouncer go through. Now there was only one ball left.

The bowler sent it down the leg side, perhaps hoping that Davey would make the same mistake as last time. On this occasion, however, Davey turned on his foot and switched his hands as if he'd been doing it since he was born. He swung Kaboom and hooked the ball high into the air. It flew towards the boundary and over.

'Six! SIX!' This time Kaboom didn't leap out of his hands and make a bow, nor did the

fielders transmogrify into seagulls. This
time, it was for real. Davey Warner had done
a switch hit for six.

The Sluggers had won.

'No-o-o-o-o-o!' It was Mo. Now he *did* look
like a pufferfish.

That afternoon, Sunil and Davey were lying
on the grass in the backyard sucking
on Whopper Chomps and discussing the
morning's events.

'I lined up Lata to put bi-carb soda on their
oranges,' Sunil admitted. 'I was hoping it
might react with the acid in the oranges and
make them froth. Thought that might freak
out the Crickets and put them off their game.
But it just made their oranges taste weird.'

'*Our* oranges, you mean. She did it to *our* oranges.' Davey gave his friend a kick with his good leg.

'Mmm, that's what I thought too.' Sunil looked a little remorseful. 'Actually, Lata did put it on *their* oranges, while everyone was chasing Max around the field. But Mo saw her do it and as soon as she walked away, he switched them with ours.'

'How do you know?'

'He couldn't wait to tell me, as soon as I got out. He also told me how much he enjoyed seeing me go down for a golden duck.'

'Yeah, I guess he would have liked that.'

Sunil grinned. 'That's okay. I'll get him back another day. And anyway, thanks to your secret weapon, we won, which Mo must have hated even more. Ha!'

'Sunil! Are you ready?' Lata was peering over the top of the fence.

'Okay.' He sat up and dusted himself off. 'I've got to go. Things to do.'

'You're not cooking up more secret weapons, I hope,' Davey said.

'Nah, I promised to teach Lata her times tables. She already knows some of them,' Sunil said proudly.

'Lucky Lata,' Davey said. 'After all, you're such an *expert*.'

'True.' Sunil stood and stretched, then headed down the side path. 'Watch out!' he called. 'Here comes Max the Axe!'

Davey heard a bark. Max appeared. Zipping across the grass, the dog jumped on Davey and licked his face.

'Get off!' Davey gave the dog a push. 'Aaarrgghh! What have you been rolling in? You stink!'

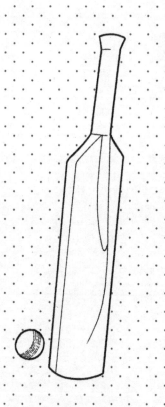

CHAPTER 14

WELCOME TO KINDY CRICKET SPECTACULAR

In the end, the Welcome to Kindy showcase turned out better than Davey and his friends expected. Even though they felt silly in marsupial makeup and headbands with ears, and despite the fact that everyone said they looked more like bush rats than kangaroos, it was fun to be something other than eleven-year-old boys for a few hours.

Davey had to admit that nice Ms Maro had done a good job. There were stalls selling cakes and drinks and funny signs telling people where to go and what to do. She'd even managed to convince the teachers to dress up as Australian animals, which seemed to put them in a better mood.

When Mr Mudge appeared in a giant sugar glider costume, Davey nearly fell off his crutches. The usually grumpy teacher was only surpassed by Mrs Trundle, who looked almost approachable as a ringtail possum.

Davey did feel a bit sorry for the kindy kids, who probably thought that school was going to be like this every day from here on. *Just you wait*, he thought.

Sunil and Davey were loitering by the cake stall when Ms Maro bustled over in her quokka costume. 'Come on, boys. Time to set up for the cricket display. Davey, will you be okay on those crutches?'

Davey nodded. 'They're just for show now, Miss. And to keep Mum happy.'

'Well, that's the most important thing.' She flashed him a big smile. She really did have the loveliest eyes, Davey thought.

While Ms Maro and some Year Six quolls directed people to their seats, the cricketers set up and took their positions. At the same time, the choir of echidnas filed onto the temporary stage.

Ms Maro spoke a few words of welcome, then Bella grabbed the microphone. 'I'm Bella Ferosi, school captain and the choir's lead soprano,' she said, giving her echidna spines a flick. 'Today we're singing the school song. It's called "Give Your Best – If Possible", after the school motto.'

Sunil gave a friendly wave in the direction of the choir. 'Check out Clouter,' he whispered.

Davey glanced over. Mo stood in the middle of the back row, his shoulders slumped and teeth bared. His furry ears were lopsided and his nose had smudged. He looked like the most miserable echidna ever born.

The choir burst into song, but Davey could tell even from a distance that Mo wasn't singing. For one thing, his mouth didn't move once.

When the singing was over and the applause had died down, it was time for the bandicoot gymnasts. Once the last vault had been executed, the lawn bowls team trooped onto the grass beside the stage.

As the team played a mock tournament, Mr Mudge gave a commentary.

Once again, Davey thought how slow and dull the game seemed, but the kids were genuinely enjoying it. As for Mr Mudge, well, his ears glowed a rosy peach as he described every move of the players and explained the rules.

'There's nothing like it,' he concluded. 'Skill, luck, strategy, action, excitement. It's all of these rolled into one glossy, beautiful bowling ball of a game.' Davey saw Mr Mudge glance at Mrs Trundle. 'Wouldn't you agree?'

Mrs Trundle's eye hadn't twitched all morning and it didn't start now. Instead, she smiled. 'Mr Mudge, you have taken the words right out of my mouth.'

At that moment, Ms Maro stepped forward. 'Thank you, Mr Mudge, Mrs Trundle. Now I have the pleasure of introducing the school cricket team. And what a team they are!' She looked across at the cricketers. 'Okay, guys, hit it!'

As planned, Sunil bowled to George, who hit it neatly to Kevin, who caught it on the bounce, and George ran for one. Sunil bowled an inswinger to Ivy, who hit it neatly to Talia at cover, who threw it to Kevin, who came in to bowl. Kevin's leg break went through, as intended, to Dylan, the keeper, who stumped George, at which point Davey tossed his crutches aside and ran to the crease with Kaboom. As previously agreed, Kevin bowled a flipper. Davey spun like a ballerina, swapped his hands and performed his amazing switch hit as if he were playing for Australia.

The ball sailed through the air like a heat-seeking missile. It grazed Mr Mudge's left ear, which spontaneously turned from peach to purple. But just as Mr Mudge was about to explode, the crowd cheered.

'Out!' It was Mo. He was standing by the cake stall and had managed to get his hands to the ball. But already he was toppling backwards. With a crash, he fell into the cakes and dropped the ball, sending cupcakes, muffins and toffees flying in every direction.

The kindy kids had been sitting quietly on the mats at the front watching the display. Now they jumped to their feet and ran laughing and shouting after the baked goods.

While the parents and teachers rounded up the kindies and cakes, Ms Maro helped the cricketers and bowlers put away their gear. 'That was a wonderful display,' she said to Sunil and Davey, as they packed the wickets and bails into carry cases.

'Thanks, Miss. Glad you enjoyed it,' Sunil said.

'You boys won't know what to do with yourselves, now you're finished with detention, will you?' There was sympathy in Ms Maro's voice.

Sunil smiled so his dimple showed. 'Guess not. What'll we do, Warner?'

'Not sure. Play lawn bowls, I guess.'

'Mr Mudge and Mrs Trundle certainly enjoy it,' Ms Maro said, her brown eyes sparkling. 'You might find you like it.'

Sunil shrugged. 'Maybe.'

'Hmmm.' Davey looked up at Ms Maro. 'You never know,' he said, smiling.

But he did know. Cricket was his game, and it always would be. For one thing, in lawn bowls they didn't use bats. What kind of game was that? And how could he possibly play a game without Kaboom?

It wasn't worth thinking about.

Playing Up

DAVID WARNER

with **J.S. BLACK,** Illustrated by **JULES FABER**

SIMON & SCHUSTER
AUSTRALIA
A CBS COMPANY

FOR STEVE

CONTENTS

CHAPTER 1

SIX AND OUT STEVE

Davey Warner gripped the worn red cricket ball in his hand. His thumb traced the rough seam in the cracked leather before he found the right grip. He gave his shoulders a stretch and jogged lightly on the spot.

'Game on,' Davey said quietly to himself.

As if responding to Davey's comment, the batsman at the other end of the pitch tapped the crease with the end of his bat and waited. His expression was of fierce concentration.

Davey found his mark and turned. 'Let's see how you like this one,' he muttered.

He came in a few paces off a short run and released his leg-break. But it pitched short of a length and a loud 'whack!' sounded. Davey watched as the ball sailed over his head to the outer.

What a cracker! Davey's dog Max yelped and then tore off after the ball.

'Stink!' Davey pulled a face.

Davey's older brother, Steve, looked far too pleased with his shot. 'You need to mix it up more,' he said to Davey. 'Try one that comes straight on.'

'Yeah, yeah,' Davey muttered.

It was Sunday afternoon and even though Davey had already played two games of cricket that weekend he was keen for more. Only trouble was, Steve was hitting him to all parts of the backyard *and* kept giving him unasked-for coaching tips. It was driving Davey bonkers.

Max loved nothing more than fielding for the Warner brothers. He'd retrieve ball after ball relentlessly, dropping it each time at Davey's feet in a slobbery pile.

'Hurry up, Max,' Davey called. He was itching to get his brother out.

Max let out a series of excited whines as he searched frantically through the overgrown shrubbery alongside the back fence.

'I can see how you're holding the ball, so I know how you're going to bowl,' Steve told Davey as they wandered over to help Max in his search. 'You want to keep the ball hidden from the batter.'

'Der, I know!' Davey had just about heard enough of Steve's advice.

Steve shrugged and said nothing. He was fourteen and captain of the Sandhill Saints. Davey knew that Steve loved cricket just as much as he did, but Steve didn't always love playing with his little brother. The feeling was mutual – Davey preferred to play cricket with his friends Sunil, Kevin and George. For one thing, they didn't tell him what to do.

Steve found the ball and after giving it a quick rub to remove most of the slobber he tossed it to Davey. They went back to their positions and Max moved to silly mid-on and crouched low. *You won't get it past me this time*, he seemed to say.

Davey ran in, trying hard to hide his grip. It felt awkward and he served up a full toss that Steve hooked to the fence for four.

'Double stink!' he cursed.

'Don't lose it, Davey,' Steve called when he saw the dark look on Davey's face. 'You can't just rely on your batting. You need to be able to bowl as well.'

'Yes, oh Great One.' Davey rolled his eyes. 'You aren't exactly Shane Warne yourself.'

He jogged over to the side fence that separated their house from his best friend Sunil's. Davey had lost count of how many runs Steve would have scored over the last hour.

Davey lined up at the end of his run-up for the next ball and tried to clear his head, but just as he was about to let rip his brother interrupted him again.

'Concentrate on line and length,' Steve shouted.

Davey slowed down and focused on controlling his delivery.

'That's too short,' Steve said, smacking it to the off side.

Davey tried again.

'That's too full,' Steve said, driving it back over Davey's head.

Max raced for the ball *again* with a delighted yap. He hadn't seen so much action in years!

'I'd concentrate on your spinners, if I were you,' Steve said as Davey approached.

'I'd put a sock in it if I were you.' Davey bowled the next ball as fast as he could but it was over-pitched, and Steve sent it flying over the fence.

'Great shot!' Steve threw his bat into the air.

But his delight was interrupted by a high-pitched squeal followed by a loud crash and the sound of something shattering.

'Davey Warner!' Sunil's mum shouted from the other side of the fence.

Davey pulled a face. 'Sorry, Mrs Deep!'
he called. 'Look what you've done!' he hissed
at Steve.

He jogged over to where Kaboom, his
cricket bat, lay on the grass, waiting. 'Six and
out. My turn to bat.'

But Steve was already wandering towards
the house. 'I've got to meet Danny and Jerome
for practice. 'We've got the big game against
Shimmer Bay Skiffs on Saturday.'

'No way!' Davey shouted, holding up
Kaboom. *My turn to bat!*'

'See you later, little brother.' Steve ruffled
Davey's hair when he walked past him.

'David?' Mrs Deep was peering over the
fence. She waved a broom in the air. 'I'm
waiting!'

'Steve!' Davey called again, but his brother had already gone. *Typical.*

'Coming, Mrs Deep!' he called. At least he wouldn't have to hear any more of Steve's 'advice'.

Davey looked at Max. 'You stay here,' he said. But the dog was already dashing down the side path ahead of him.

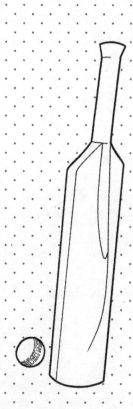

CHAPTER 2

ROUND ONE TO MUDGE

Davey gazed out of the classroom window
at the dusty playing fields. He squirmed
restlessly on the hard wooden seat. It was
a brilliantly still summer's day – perfect
conditions for cricket. In fact, it was perfect
conditions for anything *other* than listening to
grumpy old Mr Mudge drone on relentlessly

with algebra questions while Davey's whole class – 6M, for 'Mudge' – nodded off.

'A boat is travelling at a constant speed for five hours, covering a total distance of 338.49 kilometres. How fast was it going?' Mudge asked in a monotone.

This is torture, Davey thought. *Does he really expect anyone to answer?*

Davey's mind drifted off to cricket, and he pictured himself at the crease, leaning into his bat, Kaboom. The ball came fast and straight. The crowd 'Ooh-ed' when they realised the ball was rocketing straight for his face, but he didn't even flinch. Judging it perfectly, Davey struck it and with a mighty crack sent it flying high over square leg and then the boundary for six.

The crowd erupted! 'Warner! Warner!' they chanted, cheering their hero.

Davey nodded and smiled, soaking up the adulation. Cricket glory, fans, playing for a rep side – it was all within his reach. Davey and his bat Kaboom were going places.

'Warner!' a familiar, cranky voice snapped Davey out of his daydream. '*What* is so amusing?'

Davey came back to earth with a painful thud. Mr Mudge's face was just centimetres from his own. The teacher didn't look happy, and his ears, which peeked out from under lank wisps of grey hair, were rapidly turning a shocking pink.

Davey remembered – maths. 'Yes, Sir?' he asked innocently.

'We're waiting for the answer, Warner,' Mudge drawled.

The answer? Davey didn't even know the question. Something to do with a boat? He looked at the board for clues but it was just a mass of squiggles and equations. He made a show of studying his notes, but the page in front of him was full of cricket bat designs.

Mudge crossed his arms impatiently. 'We're waiting.'

Just as Davey opened his mouth, there was a knock at the classroom door.

'Saved by the bell, Warner.' Mudge scowled at Davey. 'Don't move a muscle. I'll be back.'

The school principal was standing in the doorway.

Mudge gave her a welcoming smile. 'Lavinia – I mean, Mrs Trundle! What can I do for you?' He hurried over to join her and they were soon deep in conversation.

'Phew!' Davey stretched out his legs in front of him.

Davey still had sore muscles from a weekend of cricket. His foot kicked his backpack, which was on the floor in front of him. Davey knew that sticking out of his bag was his cricket bat, Kaboom. It was his lucky bat and had been signed by two of his heroes, Ricky Ponting and Shane Warne. The signatures were important to Davey – if he was in a tight spot on the field, he would think of his heroes and it would help him find his focus.

Davey's hands itched to touch the willow. He glanced at Mudge. Davey could have sworn he saw him blush, although it was hard to tell, because the teacher's ears had changed back from shocking pink to just pink.

Mudge was still laughing and talking to Mrs Trundle. Davey could hear snatches of conversation about, *yawn,* lawn bowls and, *double yawn,* class grading.

Davey pulled out his bat and held it in his hands.

'Hi, Kaboom,' Davey said quietly.

Kaboom was made from beautifully balanced English willow. Davey had put on his own grip and he oiled the bat carefully at the start of the season, giving the face and edges extra care and attention. It was well worn in now, especially since it had so many dents and cherries from hitting sixes out of the park.

The call to play was bigger than Davey, and he just couldn't help himself. He slipped out of his seat and adopted a stance at the crease, demonstrating one of his favourite shots, the square cut.

He looked around at his friends Sunil, George and Kevin, who were each sitting in different corners of the room, specifically so they couldn't talk about cricket all day. 'This is how Ricky would deal with a short ball outside the off stump,' Davey whispered rather loudly.

Sunil scrunched up a piece of paper into a tight ball and pitched it across the room to Davey.

Every other student in 6M watched in silent awe as the paper ball flew high into the air. It seemed to move in slow motion as it bounced off the top of Mudge's balding head and landed on the floor beside him.

Davey sucked in a breath. *Uh-oh!*

'Now you've done it,' said Bella Ferosi, the school captain who sat next to Davey. Her brown ponytail flicked back and forth as she looked from Mudge to the soon-to-be-shark-bait Warner.

'Warrr-nerrr!' If Mudge had been blushing before, he now looked set to blow a fuse. His ears had gone purple, and crimson red blotches had appeared all over his face.

'You're dead meat, Shorty.' Mo Clouter sat on Davey's other side and was perhaps Davey's least-favourite person.

Mrs Trundle's eye twitched. Davey knew that meant she was about to lose it. Clearly unimpressed, she quickly took her leave, but not before throwing Mudge a look that could have killed a cat.

Mudge turned on Davey. 'When I get my hands on you, Warr-nerrr . . .' he spluttered and tiny sparks shot out of his ears.

Davey held Kaboom out in front of him in mock defence.

'Give it here.' Mudge reached a hand out for the bat.

'Ah, this is my lucky charm, Sir,' Davey said. 'I can't play cricket without it.'

'GIVE IT TO ME!' Mudge spat out the words with such force that little bobbles of spit flew from his mouth and landed on Davey's shirt.

'Please, Sir! I'll do detention, anything . . .' Davey pleaded.

'The bat!' Mudge grabbed hold of Kaboom and pulled.

But Davey couldn't let go. It wasn't that he was a show-off, but Kaboom was his most prized possession. Together, Davey and his bat had plans. They'd made a pact to not only win the season but to show the selectors the art of batting and that they had a place on the rep side.

Mr Mudge didn't see it quite the same way. 'Let it go,' he seethed.

There was a short and vicious tug of war before Davey finally gave up. Mudge cleared his throat, smoothed a strand of oily hair over his scalp and placed the bat on his desk with a clunk that made Davey wince.

George, Kevin and Sunil gave Davey looks of sympathy.

'How long will you have it, Sir?' Davey asked meekly as he sat down.

'Not sure, Warner,' Mudge said. 'Long enough.'

Mo sniggered. 'You gonna cry now, Shorty?'

Davey slid down low in his seat. He hated to admit it, but for once the boneheaded bully was right. He did feel like crying.

CHAPTER 3

NO KABOOM GLOOM

'I can't believe I've been out-Mudged by Mudge,' Davey said glumly.

Davey opened his lunchbox, stared at the contents and replaced the lid. He was usually starving by lunchtime, but today he was too churned up about Kaboom to eat.

'He's really got you by the goolies,' Sunil agreed, crunching on an apple. He dug in his bag and held another one out to Davey, who shook his head.

George, Sunil, Kevin and Davey were eating lunch in their usual spot near the row of oleanders which lined the school playgrounds. It meant they could eat and then get back to playing cricket, which was how they usually spent their lunch hours – rain, hail or shine.

'How long do you reckon Mudge'll keep Kaboom?' Davey asked.

'He confiscated Anh Nguyen's trick yo-yo for six months,' George said.

'And he still has Luca Panas's game cards,' Sunil added.

'So, like forever?' Davey groaned. 'That's the rest of the season!'

He fell back on the grass and closed his eyes. Then he remembered. 'We've got training this arvo.' He sat up abruptly. 'What am I going to do?'

'You can borrow my bat,' George said.

'Thanks, Pepi.' Davey sighed. He appreciated the offer, but no bat in the world could replace Kaboom. Davey knew the bat so well it was like an extension of his own body. It was as if Mudge had cut off his left arm.

'I got a bad case of the Mo Clouter blues,' Kevin murmured.

Davey looked up to see Mo and his friends, Nero and Tony, approaching. The best way Davey had found to deal with the meatheads was to ignore them. Davey lay back down on the grass and closed his eyes. Before too long, Mo's hulk of a body blocked out the sun and Davey was cast into shadow.

'Oi, Shorty . . .' Mo looked down at Davey. 'What'll you do without your *lucky bat*, you poor little peanut?'

'You losing sleep over me, Mo?' Davey asked, with his eyes still closed. 'I never knew you cared.'

'Not likely,' Mo retorted. 'I never think about you cricket kooks.'

'You don't think, period,' Davey shot back at Mo.

'You'll never see your bat again!' sneered Mo.

'What would you know?' Davey replied.

'Mudge took my lucky cap a year ago and never gave it back,' Mo said bitterly.

'Thanks for the intel.'

Mo pulled a face when he saw what George was eating. 'Urgh!'

'Want one?' George offered up a lunchbox full of neatly wrapped vine leaves.

'No way!' Mo backed away. 'Freaky foreign food! Come on, boys, something smells off here.'

The hulk and his cronies ambled off.

'And we were having such a great chat,' Sunil called after them, giving them a friendly wave.

'Mo's right,' Davey said. 'Mudge will never give Kaboom back willingly. He hates cricket. He'd be loving this.'

'What can you do?' Kevin asked.

'I have to get it back myself. Whatever the punishment, I don't care. Kaboom is mine and Mudge has no business taking away my stuff.'

'Go, Warner!' Sunil said, clearly impressed.

'Where do you think he'll keep it?' Davey asked his friends.

'Staffroom?' Sunil suggested.

'Classroom?' Kevin added.

'Sports room?' George said, through a mouth full of food.

'We just have to keep looking,' Davey said. 'I'm getting Kaboom back, if it's the last thing I do!'

When Davey made up his mind about something, he stuck to it.

CHAPTER 4

MUDGE MAKEOVER

Mudge made a point of leaving Kaboom
lying on top of his desk for the rest of the day.
Confiscating Davey's bat seemed to have given
the teacher a new lease of life. He talked non-
stop all afternoon with something close to
enthusiasm.

Mo had long since drifted off, but the rest of the class were in a state of panic. Enthusiastic Mudge was even *worse* than normal Mudge. The man would just not shut up.

Davey sighed and scratched his head.

Even Bella Ferosi, who was not only school captain but 6M's most diligent student, appeared to be having trouble keeping up with Mudge as she furiously scribbled down notes.

Sunil had had enough. He shot up a hand.

'Yes, Sunil?' Mudge looked a little peeved at being interrupted.

'Uh, Sir, the bell went ten minutes ago.' Sunil smiled so that his dimple showed. 'I'd be happy to stay, but I have to get to coaching college.'

Davey rolled his eyes at his friend's ability to suck up, and Sunil shot him a sly grin.

'Look at that!' Mudge exclaimed, glancing at the clock. 'Yes, of course, Deep. Mustn't hold you kids up from your extracurricular activities!'

He dabbed at the layer of sweat on his forehead and chuckled to himself.

Kids? Davey mouthed. Mudge never called them *kids*. Monsters, abominations probably, but not kids. And he *never* agreed with them.

'Off you go, then!' Mudge called after them, with something close to affection. Who had taken Mudge away and replaced him with this imposter? Davey wondered.

Davey hung back as the rest of 6M filed out of the classroom. Sunil's fib had given Davey an idea. He'd tell Mudge that the bat belonged to his Uncle Vernon.

'Um, Sir . . .'

'No, David,' Mudge replied, without looking around while he wiped down the board. 'I have *not* changed my mind.'

'But—'

'If you take one step out of line, I'll call your mother and tell her what happened today. I'm sure she'll find it *interesting*.' Mudge hummed as he pottered around the room, tidying up.

Mmm. Not so good. Davey changed plan. 'Do you know where you'll be keeping it, Sir?' he asked casually.

Mudge turned to him and gave a wink. 'THAT is the million-dollar question, isn't it, Warner? For me to know and you to find out.'

Davey knew it was useless to argue. He abandoned the classroom and made his way over to get his bike. His mates would already be down at the beach having a hit before training.

At the bike racks, Davey found Mo, Nero and Tony blocking his way.

'Oh dear, Warner,' Mo pouted like a toddler having a tantrum. 'What are you going to do without your p-p-p-precious bat?'

Davey gritted his teeth and unlocked his bike. There was no point biting back. Anyway, he'd had enough for the day. First Mudge, and now Mo.

'Going home to have a cry?' Mo taunted.

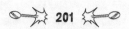

Davey paused. There were a few comebacks lining up in his head, but it would just infuriate Mo, possibly to the point of no return. *Time to dig deep*, he thought.

He looked at Mo and gave him his biggest grin. 'Not at all. I couldn't be happier, Clouter.'

Then he jumped on his bike and pedalled away without looking back.

Later, at training, Davey was unsure where to begin without Kaboom. He hung back as the others sorted themselves into positions and began to practise. Their coach Benny hadn't arrived, but that wasn't unusual. Benny *showing up* to training would be more unusual.

'Want to use my bat?' Sunil offered. He had a beautiful Kookaburra bat that he polished obsessively.

Davey knew it was a big thing for Sunil to lend his bat to anyone. But Davey shook his head. It wasn't the same.

'Nah, I'll bowl.' He grabbed his ball from his school bag and headed to the other wicket. 'Steve, the know-it-all cricket oracle, reckons I need the practice, anyway.'

'Let's see what you've got then, Warner,' Sunil said. He grabbed his bat and took up his position at the crease.

Davey gave the ball a quick rub against his thigh. He might as well take Steve's advice and concentrate on his leg-spinners. He couldn't always rely on his batting – especially now he was Kaboomless. *Being*

a better bowler will make me a better batter,
he told himself.

As Davey did a few arm warm-ups, Steve's
advice kept coming back to him: *Concentrate
on getting the ball to the right place.* But leg-
spinners were really difficult to get right.

After a few warm-up bowls, Davey was
still finding it hard to get the ball in the right
spot. He bowled to George next, but it was
too short and George pulled it square. The
next ball was too full and wide and George
smacked it through the off side.

'Come on, Warner!' George called out.
'Give us a hard one!'

Finally Davey landed the ball in the right
spot. It turned and beat George, knocking
over his off stump.

'Ah!' That felt a little better.

'Way to go!' Sunil shouted.

'Over here, boys!' Benny was standing on the edge of the park, bags of equipment at his feet.

'Only half an hour late,' George said to the others. 'Not bad for Benny.'

The boys wandered over. Benny was puffed from lugging all the gear a good two metres from his car.

'Sorry I'm late,' he said, scratching his scalp. Davey watched as white flakes tumbled onto his shoulders and rested there in a snowy patch.

While the team gathered around him, Benny took a moment to catch his breath. 'I've got some news,' he announced, a quiver of excitement in his voice.

Davey's ears pricked up. He caught Sunil's eye. He also looked as if he was eager to hear what Benny had to say.

'I've been given a heads-up that a regional selector is keen to come along this week to take a look at you all,' Benny said.

'Yes!' Davey punched the air. It was the news they'd been waiting for all season.

'That's awesome!' George said.

'Don't get your hopes up,' Benny added quickly, with a look of commiseration. 'The chances of any of you lot getting picked are pretty close to zero. It's always best to aim low in my experience,' he concluded, farting at the same time.

Despite the pong, the team immediately broke into excited chatter. Even Benny's usual pessimism couldn't take the shine off the news. A selector coming to watch them meant that they were on the lookout for new talent for the local rep side. It was the moment Davey had been waiting for. The news was huge.

'When will he be here?' Sunil asked.

'Tomorrow night,' Benny continued, 'so we'll do an extra training night this week. Make sure you're all on time,' he said, waggling a sausage finger at them.

That was rich coming from Benny, thought Davey. The last time he turned up on time was probably 1985.

'This is my chance!' Sunil sucked in his breath, his eyes glassy with excitement.

'Dream on, Deep,' George said. 'It's me they'll want.'

 207

Sunil rolled his eyes. 'Only if they need someone to do the drinks run. Then you'd be a shoo-in.'

George silenced his friend with a look.

Mudge couldn't have picked a worse week to ruin Davey's life. Without Kaboom, what hope did he have for impressing anybody?

'Boys, we need a plan.' Davey drew the others in close to him. 'I've got to have Kaboom back in time for tomorrow night. Otherwise I'm cactus.'

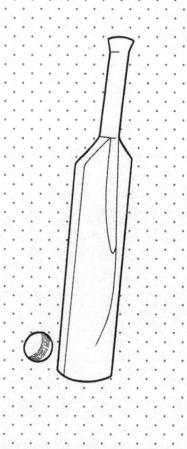

CHAPTER 5
FACING THE MUSIC

It was dark by the time Davey wheeled his bike up the side path. He crossed his fingers and prayed that Mr Mudge hadn't called his mum to tell her about the bat. If Mudge *had* told her, Davey would be in BIG trouble – so much trouble, in fact, that he might as well turn around and leave home, never to return.

Davey knew his mum would freak if she found out that Kaboom had been confiscated – for two reasons. The first was, well . . . Davey could hear her now: *You were playing cricket in class? And Mr Mudge got hit in the head! What were you thinking?*

The second reason was that the bat had been a very special birthday present from his parents and granddad. If his mum found out, she'd think he didn't know how to look after his stuff. *Looks like we won't be buying you any more serious presents like that again,* she'd say. And even worse: *Granddad's very disappointed!*

Max appeared around the corner and tore down the path towards him, barking and wagging his tail furiously.

'Max, you're a menace,' Davey said, giving the dog a rough scratch behind the ears.

Pushing past his dog, he wheeled his bike around the back and looked up at the house. All seemed quiet, but then, that didn't mean anything.

'Is Mum home?'

Max cocked his head. *You'll find out*, he seemed to say. He wasn't giving anything away. After all, Davey's mum fed him!

'Mmm.' Davey got the hint. 'No cracking you, Mr Mutt,' he said. 'All right, where's the ball?'

At the mention of the word 'ball', Max jumped up on his hind legs and did a little dance.

'Here you go.' Davey pulled a ball from his bag and pelted it to the far end of the yard.

Max took off at lightning speed. He launched himself at the rolling ball, grabbed it in his teeth, turned a one-eighty and charged back towards Davey.

It was a perfectly timed routine. Just as Davey bent down to pick up the ball, Max dropped the slobbery article at his feet.

'Let's see what you think about this one!' Davey took a run-up and came hurtling towards Max.

'Mix it up, keep it on a length . . .' he said, mimicking his brother, before firing a googly at the imaginary batsman.

Max yelped in admiration and raced after the ball.

'Not bad,' said a voice.

Davey swung around in surprise.

Steve was slouched against the frame of the back door. 'Dinner's ready,' he said.

Davey climbed the back stairs. 'Is Mum home?'

'Yep,' Steve said. 'She cooked it.'

Davey dropped his voice so his mum wouldn't overhear. 'I'm in a bit of trouble,' he whispered to Steve. 'I was mucking around and, well, Kaboom got confiscated.'

'Let me guess . . . Mudge?' Steve laughed.

Davey nodded.

'Mum'll *freak*!' Steve exclaimed a little too loudly.

'Shh!'

'I won't dob, if that's what you're worried about.'

'Boys, dinner's ready!' their mum called.

'Do you think she knows?' Davey asked. He peered anxiously through the open door, trying to get a glimpse of the expression on his mother's face.

Steve shrugged. 'Better get inside.'

'Hang on . . .' Davey said. 'Can I use your bat?'

'Mate, no way!' Steve held up his hands in protest. 'We've got the game against the Skiffs this weekend, and practice is on every night.'

'I forgot about that,' Davey mumbled, disappointed.

'Anyway, you should practise with lots of different bats. You shouldn't just rely on one.' Steve was giving advice *again*.

'Quit it, will you?' Davey snapped. 'I don't want other bats. I want my bat!'

'Down, boy!' Steve backed away. 'Cool it.'

'Benny says a selector might turn up tomorrow night,' Davey muttered.

'Seriously?' Steve asked. 'Well, it's still good advice. You don't want to be scared in a game just 'cause you don't have the perfect equipment. You've got to mix it up.'

'Scared? I'm not *scared* of anything!' Davey had heard enough of Steve's advice to last until the year 2065.

'David and Steven Warner!' their mum shouted in a shrill voice. 'For the last time, DINNER IS READY!'

The boys looked at each other in alarm.

Davey grimaced. 'Well, apart from Mum sometimes . . .'

The two brothers hurried inside.

CHAPTER 6
CAUGHT OUT

'I've never been at school this early before,'
Kevin said as they entered the school grounds.
There were only one or two students on the
near-empty playgrounds. 'It's like a ghost
town.'

'McKinley's always early,' Sunil said, 'and lucky for you blokes she *lurves* me.' He flashed his best dimpled smile.

After Benny's announcement, Sunil had done some fast thinking and come up with a plan for them to find Mudge's hiding place for Davey's bat.

'*Please,*' Davey said, 'just lead the way, lady-killer.'

'Watch and learn.' Sunil smirked as they approached the admin office.

Operation Kaboom was a go.

Sunil approached the desk of Mrs McKinley, Head of Administration, while the others waited just inside the doorway. McKinley wore coke-bottle thick glasses and was so old that nobody at school remembered a time when she hadn't worked there. Despite looking a little like a bilby, she wasn't a bad old stick.

Sunil cleared his throat. 'Good morning, Mrs McKinley!' he said brightly.

'Is that you, Mr Deep?' Mrs McKinley leant forward and peered at Sunil through her glasses.

'Yes!' Sunil smiled so his dimple showed. 'Mr Mudge has asked for another forty copies of the band excursion form, please.'

Mrs McKinley shook her head and waggled a finger. 'That Mr Mudge! He does keep me busy.'

'Don't I know it!' Sunil joked.

Davey felt a teensy bit bad about hoodwinking McKinley. She might be ancient, but she was always kind.

'I know that one.' Mrs McKinley shuffled off in slow motion to find the file. 'Pink, if I remember correctly.'

'Thank you,' Sunil crooned.

She licked a finger and selected a piece of pink paper from the top of the pile. 'All right, dear.' She shuffled off down the hall. 'I'll just copy them for you.'

Sunil waited until she was out of sight.

'Now!' Sunil whispered.

Davey, George and Kevin sprang into action. They scuttled past the office and down the corridor as Sunil joined them.

'That should buy us a few minutes,' Davey said, patting Sunil on the back.

The four boys crept towards the green door at the end of the corridor. The staffroom was strictly off limits to students. Nobody they knew had EVER tried to enter it without permission and lived to tell the tale.

Davey's mouth felt dry as Kevin cautiously opened the door a crack. He noticed Kevin's hand was shaking.

Kevin peered inside. 'All clear,' he said and entered the room. The others followed close behind.

The staffroom was brightly lit, with fluorescent light shining on every desk surface. Around the sink area there were dog-eared signs about washing up on the wall and reminders about rosters. But a quick look around the room revealed no Kaboom in sight.

'Cupboards!' Davey moved at lightning speed across the room and began to open the built-ins that lined one wall. They scoured every available storage area, but all they found were odd mugs, plates and cake platters.

'Zilch,' George said.

'We'd better get out of here.' Sunil glanced at the clock on the wall, 'McKinley's not *that* slow.'

Davey was disappointed, but he nodded.

'Er, guys . . .' George pointed to the door.

The door handle was turning. Davey looked around for somewhere to hide, but there was nowhere. On impulse, he bobbed down behind a table and pulled Sunil down with him.

'I know you're in here,' said a familiar voice as the door opened. It was Mudge.

'Holy moly.' George sucked in his breath. 'We're done for.'

Mudge glared at them. Gone was the jolly teacher from the day before. Back was the cranky teacher they knew so well.

'What do we have here? The staffroom is OUT OF BOUNDS for students!' Mudge thundered, entering the room and stopping in front of Davey and Sunil. Davey studied his long white socks and hairy knobbly knees. He stood up slowly.

'There's a really good explanation for this, S-S-Sir,' Davey stammered. His mind raced. He was so dead they may as well have buried him right there.

'I'm all ears, Warner.' Mudge was seething. His ears had gone such a dark shade of purple they were almost black.

'My bat, Sir . . . The selector . . .' Davey's voice trailed off.

'Yes?' Mudge snapped. 'All I hear about is this bat, bat, bat! One of the things that annoys me most about cricket is the confounded bat!'

'Sir, I need it to play,' Davey tried again to explain.

'Warr-ner, you will be lucky if you *ever* see your stupid cricket bat again!'

Davey's eyes widened in horror. He was speechless.

'It's just . . . please, Mr Mudge,' Sunil pleaded, 'there's a selector coming to our cricket practice tonight. It's a big deal.'

'Could you just give me my bat back for the night?' Davey asked, his eyes wide. 'And then you can lock it up.'

Mudge's eyes narrowed, and his cheeks grew more and more crimson.

'I'm sorry, boys, but you're confusing me with someone who CARES!' he exploded.

The boys stared at the floor in silence.

'AND I'll be calling your mother now to tell her that your bat will be in my possession for some time,' Mudge added with satisfaction.

'No!' Davey cried.

'No?' Mudge raised an eyebrow.

'Sir,' Davey mumbled.

Mudge rocked back and forth on his loafers. 'Now you lot can join me for rubbish duty for the, let's see—' He made a show of pondering. 'I think before school and lunchtime for the rest of the term ought to do it!' He grinned.

'But—'

'No buts, Warner!' Mudge stomped a clumpy foot for emphasis. 'Now, *scoot*!'

'Sir,' each of the boys mumbled as they filed past their teacher.

'I think Mrs McKinley wants a word with you all,' Mudge added, as he frog-marched them out of the staffroom. 'For some reason,

she has forty extra band forms photocopied for me. You wouldn't know anything about that, would you, Deep?'

Sunil shook his head and made his way down to the office to face the music.

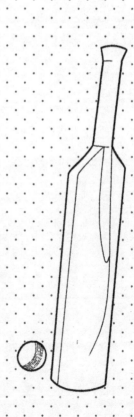

CHAPTER 7

SELECTOR REJECTOR

That night, George, Davey and Sunil gathered with the rest of the Sandhill Sluggers for the extra training session at Flatter Park. As yet there was no sign of Benny, or the so-called selector.

Davey was anxious. They all were – a mixed concoction of nerves and excitement.

Davey decided to take Steve's advice. He needed to try using other bats and improve his batting that way. He had no Kaboom, so he might as well use the next best thing.

'Can I change my mind and try your bat, Deep?' he said to Sunil.

'Thought you'd never ask!' Sunil pulled his Kookaburra out of his kit. It was a heavier bat than Kaboom, and to Davey the weight and balance felt completely different. He ran his hand down the length of the bat, getting to know it. Like Kaboom, it had a history of the games Sunil had played imprinted in dents and marks along the willow.

Davey took a swing at an imaginary ball. It felt strange to him, so he adjusted his grip on the handle and swung again. This time he overbalanced and nearly fell.

'Get a grip, Warner!' he muttered to himself. 'This is embarrassing!'

Davey got George to give him a few throw downs, to get the feel and see if he could find the sweet spot. Then he walked out to the crease and tried to find a stance that felt just right.

'Ready?' Sunil called from the bowler's end.

'Born ready,' Davey quipped as he moved into position.

Davey and Sunil had been playing cricket together for years and knew each other's tricks. But for the first time in a long time Davey felt unsure of himself as a batter. But he wasn't going to let Sunil know that.

Sunil ran in fast and Davey saw the tell-tale flick of his wrist. He shifted his position for the speed of the ball, but felt slow and clumsy. Sunil's fast ball seemed to fizz off the pitch and Davey just managed to jam his bat down and keep it out.

'Nice one!' Sunil shouted.

It had been a complete fluke, but it gave Davey a little boost of confidence. The bat felt so alien that he needed to change almost everything about the way he played.

'I'll get you this time,' Sunil said.

'I'm shaking, Deep,' Davey replied. He nodded to Sunil to let him know he was ready. He lined himself up and focused on positive thinking. *Just think about the ball*, he told himself.

'Prepare to eat dirt,' Sunil called out.

Sunil was on fire. He surprised Davey with another fast yorker and Davey played right over it. It cannoned into his stumps, clean bowling him.

'What the . . . ?' Davey was dazed. The ball had sizzled straight past him and he'd been too slow to even react.

'HOWZAT?!' Sunil exclaimed as he sprinted around in tight circles.

'Great ball, Sunil!' Ivy called from third slip.

Davey shook his head. He just wasn't himself. Instead, he was doing a great impersonation of how to play cricket badly.

Sunil commiserated. 'Sorry, Warner,' he said, giving his friend a slap on the back.

Davey shrugged. 'It was a great ball.'

'Well bowled, Sunil,' said Benny, who had just joined them in the middle. He turned to the man with him and added, 'He's not usually so good.'

Davey realised that Benny had arrived while they were playing and had been watching with another man – the selector. Trust Benny to turn up just as he got smashed!

'This is Rob, the selector I mentioned,' Benny said.

Davey's stomach lurched. Of all the plays for the selector to see, that would have to be the worst. Any hint of confidence Davey had got back drained away.

Benny's mobile rang as he was about to introduce Rob to each player. 'Hang on a mo, got to take this.' He wandered off, chatting into his phone.

Rob said hello to the team with a smile and they gathered around him while he scribbled a few notes on a small notepad. There was silence as they all watched him with bated breath. Rob finished writing and scanned their expectant faces.

'Nice to meet you,' Rob said, stepping forward to shake Sunil's hand. He shook all the players' hands in turn but didn't give Davey a second glance. His eyes were fixed on Sunil.

'A yorker is a hard ball to pull off,' Rob said. 'If you get it right, it can beat almost any batter.'

'Thanks,' Sunil said. He couldn't wipe the smile off his face.

Rob glanced at Davey momentarily. Davey felt his face grow hot and flush with embarrassment.

'There's probably nobody here you'd be interested in,' Benny said, then belched. He had finished his phone call and joined them again. 'The team tries hard, but let's face it, we're not very good.' Benny hoicked up his pants. Despite his round belly, Benny was a compulsive Harry Highpants.

Rob checked his watch and shook his head. 'I've seen enough thanks, Benny.' He turned to Sunil. 'Can I get your name and a phone number for your parents?' He had his notebook at the ready. 'I'd like to give them a call to have a chat about the possibility of you playing for the rep team.'

Sunil spelt out his name and gave Rob his parents' mobile numbers. 'This is my friend, Davey Warner,' he then said, stepping to the side to introduce the selector to Davey.

Rob smiled politely and fell into conversation, asking Sunil about his cricket aspirations. Davey felt like a fish out of water.

The selector hadn't even noticed him. The worst thing about it was that Davey understood why. If he was a regional selector, he wouldn't have noticed himself either. Davey was even more determined to get Kaboom back and show the selector just what he was made of.

CHAPTER 8

SNIFFER DOG SUCCESS

Davey woke with a start. It was dark outside, but he could have sworn he'd heard a noise outside his bedroom window.

He glanced at Max, who was fast asleep on Davey's bed, back legs in the air, snoring lightly.

'Some guard dog you make!' Davey nudged the dog, who rolled over and promptly went back to sleep.

Davey hopped out of bed and opened the curtains.

'Yikes!' Davey nearly fell over backwards at the sight of Sunil's face pressed right up against the window.

'Scared the life out of me,' Davey muttered.

Sunil mouthed the words '*Open up*' and held a finger to his lips. *Sunil must be up to one of his schemes*, Davey thought. He wondered what it was.

He opened the window and peered sleepily at his friend. 'It's not time for morning detention yet, is it?' Davey asked.

'I've had an idea about where Kaboom might be,' Sunil said. 'I'll tell you on the way to get Kevin and George.'

Despite being grounded *forever* for getting his bat confiscated, Davey nodded and began dressing.

'We'll need one of your shirts,' Sunil added, 'and the smellier the better.'

'Easy!' Davey handed over his training shirt from the night before. It ponged all right.

'And we need Max,' Sunil said.

Davey gave a low whistle and Max leapt to his feet. He stood alert on the bed, tail wagging, ready for action. Davey climbed out the window and joined his friend.

'Come on, dog,' Davey called to Max.

Max leapt expertly out of the window and Sunil closed it quietly behind him.

George did a sweep of the empty playground with his binoculars, taking in the surrounding quadrangle of buildings.

'The coast is clear,' he reported.

'That's because nobody in their right minds would be at school this early,' Kevin grunted.

'There's Trundle!' Kevin pointed towards the east corner of the school. 'Right on time, as usual.'

Mrs Trundle insisted on unlocking all of the classrooms in the school each morning. After completing this task, she monitored the main school gate – trying to catch out any uniform offences and generally being a nuisance.

The sound of keys jangling grew louder. Max's ears pricked up, but Kevin shot him a dirty look, willing him not to bark. For once, Max did what someone wanted him to do.

Kevin watched as Mrs Trundle unlocked the 6M classroom door.

'We've got about ten minutes before Mudge arrives for detention,' Sunil said.

The boys shot inside the classroom. They knew exactly where to look. Mudge had a large metal cabinet in which he stored a treasure trove of confiscated items.

'Check it out,' Davey said, holding up Duncan Carver's water pistol.

Sunil found Luca Panas's game cards and Mariana Larkin's comic books.

'I know that hat!' Kevin picked up an old battered footy cap.

'It's Mo's,' Sunil said.

Kevin shook off the dust and punched the cap back into shape.

'Correction,' he said with a cheeky grin, as he put the cap firmly on his head. '*Was* Mo's.'

Sunil laughed. 'I'd like to say it suits you, but Mo isn't known for his good taste.'

Max barked his agreement.

The boys rifled through all the stuff, but didn't find the cricket bat.

George opened Mudge's desk drawers and a small leather-bound book caught his eye. He picked it up and scanned the pages.

'Mudge writes poetry.'

Davey looked over George's shoulder at the book. It was love poetry. A name caught Davey's eye. Lavinia. The name Lavinia was repeated on almost every page. Lavinia? Did that mean Trundle?

An image of Mudge and Trundle kissing popped into Davey's head. 'Urgh!' he exclaimed and immediately stopped reading.

'You're up, Max.' Sunil gave the dog a scratch. Max sat on his haunches, eager to take part in the adventure. Sunil held Davey's shirt out for Max.

'Take a good whiff of Pong de Warner,' he instructed the dog.

Max obliged by taking a good sniff and wagging his tail. He jumped up on his hind legs and did his dance. *I know that smell!* he seemed to say.

'That's right, Max,' Sunil said encouragingly. 'We need you to find Davey's bat.'

Max ran around in circles and let out a series of short sharp barks. He jumped on Davey.

'Sshh, dog!' Davey hissed. 'Not me, the bat!'

Max tilted his head and froze. He had a whiff of something. He jumped down and began following his nose, zig-zagging around the room. He came to a tall coat cupboard in the corner and scratched at the door.

'He's got something!' Kevin exclaimed.

'Bingo!' Davey said.

George hastily shoved the notebook into his back pocket and joined the others. The boys clamoured to open the cupboard. Inside were three black umbrellas and a pale blue duffel bag with a wooden handle sticking out one side.

'Kaboom!' exclaimed Davey.

He reached for his beloved bat . . . just as a familiar voice spoke.

'I see you've found your bat, Warner,' Mudge said in barely more than a whisper. He stood planted in the open doorway, his magenta ears illuminated against the early morning light like a pair of wings about to take flight.

'Y-yes, S-Sir,' Davey stammered.

Mudge came over to the cupboard and slammed the door shut, narrowly missing Davey's fingers.

'Don't worry . . . I'll find a new hiding place for it,' he told them.

'Sir!' Davey said, crestfallen.

Mudge looked like the cat who'd eaten the cream. 'Your detention just got extended by another term!' He glared at Max. 'And how many times do I have to say GET THAT DOG OUT OF HERE!?'

They had been so close, but it looked like operation Kaboom was a no-go.

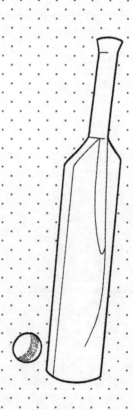

CHAPTER 9

A HAT-TRICK

The morning couldn't go quickly enough for Davey. Mudge lorded it over him by dangling Kaboom before his eyes. By the time the bell rang for lunch, Davey was desperate.

This can't be happening, he said to himself when he joined the others outside the classroom.

He didn't have Kaboom and every minute
of his life was taken up with Mudge, Mudge,
Mudge.

'You lot better be waiting when I get back,'
Mudge threatened as he went to the staffroom to
get a coffee. He'd given them ten minutes to eat
their lunch before rubbish pick-up duty began.

Kevin put on a battered old peaked cap.

'What's with the non-regulation headgear?'
Davey asked.

'Only Mo Clouter's most prized possession,'
Kevin explained with glee.

'Does he know yet?' Sunil asked.

'Any minute now.' Kevin nodded in the
direction of the quadrangle. Mo and his
entourage were approaching.

'Like my new hat, Clouter?' Kevin called.

It took a moment for Mo to register what Kevin was talking about. After all, his brain did run at a slower speed than most. Then his pimply face erupted in a scowl. He wasn't happy.

'You punk, that's my hat!' he yelled. He raced over to where Kevin stood.

'Correction. *My* hat now.'

Mo lunged at Kevin, but was too slow for Kevin's fast fielding reflexes. With lightning feet, Kevin darted to one side and easily dodged Mo's outstretched hand.

'You're going down!' Mo thundered.

'Over here!' Kevin taunted Mo by tipping his cap at him and scurrying in circles around him.

Mo was lunging at him over and over again. He kept missing by a fraction.

'Look, that's my lucky hat!' Mo growled. 'Give it here!'

'Have to catch me first,' Kevin said,  sprinting away.

Mo growled and lumbered after Kevin, chasing him around the quad. After five rounds, Mo bent over and paused to get his breath back.

'What's wrong, Mo?' Davey asked.

Mo straightened up and shook a fist at Davey.

'I'll get it back, don't you worry,' Mo snarled.

'If you say so,' Davey shot back, smiling.

Mo's face had turned purple. He was absolutely livid with rage. 'You'd better keep an eye out – all of you!' he sputtered.

He took off after Kevin again, but it was useless – Kevin was far too fast for him.

Sunil and George had tears in their eyes they were laughing so hard. But Davey had other thoughts on his mind besides Mo. As far as he was concerned, Mudge had declared war in the same way that Mo had. It was game on.

He was even more determined to get his bat back. The question was, where would Mudge hide it next?

CHAPTER 10

THE BIG SWINDLE

Davey, Sunil, George and Kevin had arrived at school early again.

The idea to look in the school sports store room had been Davey's. 'The perfect place to hide a bat is among heaps of other cricket bats,' he said.

'It's worth a shot,' George agreed.

But when they got there, the door to the store room was locked firmly with a large rusty padlock.

Davey gave it a tug, but the padlock held fast. 'So much for that idea,' he said with a sigh.

Sunil wandered around looking for a way in, but there was only one small window covered by metal bars. 'The toilets are part of the same building,' he said. 'Could we get in through them?'

Davey shrugged. 'Let's check it out.'

They went into the boys' toilets. There was a small window high above the sink that led directly into the storage room.

'You're a genius!' George gave Sunil a friendly punch.

'Better believe it,' Sunil agreed.

George studied the small opening. 'Reckon you could squeeze through?' He looked at Davey.

Davey nodded.

'I'll hoist you up.' George bent his knees and locked his hands together. Davey put one foot on George's hands and his friend gave him a lift.

'Oof!' George was rewarded with a knee in the mouth.

'Woah!' Davey wavered wildly but managed to steady himself. He reached for the ledge. 'Got it!'

'Hurry up! You're heavier than I thought,' George muttered.

'Nearly there,' Davey said through gritted teeth. He opened the tiny window a little further and, with some effort, managed to squeeze his head and his shoulders through the small opening. He was about to pull himself through, when . . .

'Someone's coming,' George hissed. 'Quick! Jump down!'

Davey tried to back out, but his shoulders were held fast. 'I can't!' he groaned. 'I'm stuck.'

He was neatly wedged in the small opening, head and shoulders on one side and his bottom and legs on the other.

'HEY!' a loud voice boomed from the doorway. 'What's going on in there?'

George, Sunil and Kevin froze as heavy footsteps echoed on the cold cement floor. Mo's ugly mug appeared around the corner. He burst out laughing.

'You should see your faces, or in your case, Shorty, your bum!' He pulled a face. 'Ooh, no! Did you think I was a teacher?'

'What do you want, Clouter?' George asked.

'I want my hat back,' Mo said with a sneer.

'Guys . . .' Davey said, 'I'm stuck.'

'I'm here to make a trade.' Mo held up a duffel bag. 'Shorty's hunk of wood for my lucky hat.'

'Where'd you find it?' George asked with suspicion. 'Mudge moved it.'

'Look, do you want it or not?' Mo sounded impatient. He dangled the bag in front of them.

'Guys,' Davey called, 'get me down!'

'Hang on,' Sunil said. He reached for the duffel bag.

'Uh uh.' Mo shook his head and held the bag just out of reach. 'Give me my hat first.'

Kevin narrowed his eyes. 'How do we know we can trust you?'

'What choice do you have? Your little friend can't play without it, can he?'

'Guys, I'll handle this,' Davey said. 'Just get me down!'

Kevin glanced at George and Sunil. They both nodded.

'All right.' Kevin held out the cap.

Mo grabbed it and put it on before dropping the duffel bag on the ground next to George. A slow smile appeared on Mo's face.

'GET ME DOWN!' Davey kicked his legs against the wall.

Sunil and Kevin each took one of Davey's legs and yanked him down.

He fell hard onto the cement floor. 'Ow!' Davey grimaced as he rubbed his shoulders.

There was silence as George unzipped the duffel bag.

'What?' Davey asked when he saw the look on George's face.

As soon as Davey saw the bat, he knew it wasn't Kaboom. With a sinking feeling, he watched George pull it out. It was ancient. Mo had probably paid fifty cents for it at a garage sale.

'You asked for it,' Mo growled.

'Where's Kaboom?' Davey was seething.

'You'll never get near it. Mudge carries it around with him all the time.' Mo leered and tipped his cap to Kevin. 'See you, suckers!' He sneered and ran off.

Davey hated to let Mo or Mudge get the better of him, but how was he ever going to get Kaboom back now?

CHAPTER 11

BATTING FOR BRADMAN

Davey sat on the back steps staring into space. Usually Friday afternoon meant cricket with the boys, but being grounded meant he was stuck at home.

He absentmindedly gave a tennis ball a rub and turned it over in his hand. Max whined

and nudged his nose up against Davey's leg, hoping he'd get the hint. The dog tucked his hind legs neatly underneath his tail and sat down. He gazed at his owner hopefully.

'Here, dog.' Davey chucked the ball across the lawn towards the back fence. He didn't even bother trying to bowl properly. His arm ached and his whole body felt heavy.

Max trotted back along the grass and dropped the wet ball at Davey's feet. He rolled it back and forth expertly with his nose and whimpered.

'No more, Max,' Davey said abruptly, then headed into the house.

Davey was rarely home this early. Normally he'd be out playing cricket with his friends until dinner time. Nobody else was home and the house felt spookily quiet.

He opened the pantry door and stared at the contents. Usually he was ravenous after school, but today nothing appealed. He closed the door and ambled into the TV room. A quick flick of the remote told him that nothing interested him.

Once inside his bedroom, Davey flopped on the bed with a sigh. He lay on his back and gazed up at the ceiling. One of the reasons he loved his bat so much was because it had been a gift from his granddad and they had spent time together sanding and oiling it to perfection. His granddad had taught him how to look after a bat – what the willow wanted and how to tell when it needed attention. He knew it would sound stupid to say out loud, but his bat was like family.

Above his bedhead was a poster of his hero, Ricky Ponting. The poster was so old and faded it had taken on a greenish tinge. Davey still loved looking at it, even if Sunil had drawn a beard on Ricky's chin and coloured in two of his teeth.

Now Davey flopped over to look at his hero. Davey could imagine Ricky yelling out to the bowler: 'Mate, is that all you've got?'

'Did you ever feel like giving up, Ricky?' Davey asked.

Ricky rearranged his cap and considered the question. *There were times when I doubted myself.*

'I know how you feel,' Davey said.

It's up to you to turn things around, Davey. Ricky looked directly at him. *Nobody else can do it for you.*

'How? I don't have my lucky bat!'

 274

Don Bradman practised without a bat and look what he did! You have to improvise, Ricky continued. *Nothing ever goes the way you want under match conditions, either. You just have to be prepared!*

And with that, Ricky gave Davey a knowing wink.

Davey thought about Ricky's advice. His brother Steve and Ricky were both saying the same thing. Davey needed to take control. He needed to stop letting cricket haters like Mudge and Mo get in his way.

Suddenly, he felt energised. 'Max!' he yelled at the top of his voice.

Max jumped up onto the bed and licked his face.

'Urgh, gross!' Davey pushed Max off the bed and got up. 'Stop slacking off, Max, we need to practise!'

Davey searched inside one of the kitchen drawers. Ricky's tip about The Don had given him an idea. He found an old golf ball of his dad's and headed outside to the pitch. Then he pulled up one of the wickets and carried it over to the side of the house.

When Steve got home half an hour later, Davey was still practising his batting using a wooden stump and hitting a golf ball repeatedly against the wall. Steve smiled and headed inside the house.

CHAPTER 12
BIG BROTHER

It was finally Saturday morning. Davey and
Sunil were in Davey's backyard having a hit.
For once there was no Sluggers game, because
they had a bye, but Davey was fired up to
practise his leg-spin bowling. It still wasn't
going well.

'I need to rip the ball more to make it spin and bounce,' Davey said. 'But it's really hard.'

Sunil was no great shakes as a batter, but he was having no problem dealing with Davey's gentle leggies, especially as Davey couldn't maintain a consistent length.

'Yeah, you should bowl more often!' Sunil agreed. 'I've never batted so well!' With that, he gave Max another four to retrieve.

'It's only spinning one way,' Davey said, thinking out loud. 'I'm going to have to learn to bowl a wrong'un like Shane Warne.'

'You've got to do something, Warner,' Sunil said with a grin, ''cause this is just too easy.'

Davey made a Mo Clouter face. 'You could live to regret those words!'

'Watch me,' Sunil retorted, waiting. 'Let's face it, you have the ugliest bowling action I've ever seen!'

Davey went back to his mark. He gripped the ball tightly, came in off his short run and ripped the ball as hard as he could. It pitched just outside leg stump. For once it bounced and spun viciously.

'Take that!'

Sunil was beaten. He pushed forward and only succeeded in edging the ball to where first slip would normally stand. Max had been waiting at mid-off and collected the ball between his jaws before dropping it back to Davey.

'Hmmf,' Sunil said.

'I've still got it!' Davey gloated.

'I bet you can't do that again,' Sunil said.

'Bet you I can!'

Davey was getting his groove back. As he walked back to his mark, he noticed Steve coming out of the house. He was wearing his cricket whites.

Max let out a happy yap and raced over to Steve.

'No more advice, bro!' Davey said, bristling. 'I'm doing everything you told me.'

Steve laughed. 'Good! Because we need you.'

'Who needs me?'

'The Sandhill Saints,' Steve said. 'We've got the big game against Shimmer Bay Skiffs.'

Davey had forgotten about Steve's big game. He would give anything to watch it and support Steve, even if he was the world's most annoying older brother.

'Have you forgotten, I'm grounded, for . . . like, *ever*,' Davey said.

'You can come,' Steve said. 'I cleared it with Mum.'

'You did?' Davey was taken aback. This was news.

'We need an eleventh man,' Steve explained. 'Lee Woon's injured.'

'You want *me*?' Davey was floored.

Steve dug his index finger into Davey's chest. 'We want you.'

'Way to go, Warner!' Sunil slapped his mate on the back.

Davey was taken aback. 'I thought . . . I thought you didn't think I was any good.'

'You're *okay*,' Steve said with a grin. 'Not bad for an eleven-year-old.'

'High praise from the master!' Davey did a mock bow.

'Don't let it go to your head,' Steve warned.

Davey beamed. He was still stunned at the news. Playing for the under-fourteens. That was massive! His mind raced.

'Hurry up and grab your stuff,' Steve said. 'Game starts in an hour. Danny's mum is going to pick us up in about ten minutes.'

Steve headed back inside, leaving the two friends staring at each other.

'Lucky you, Warner,' Sunil said. 'You never know, that selector could be there to watch.'

Davey remained rooted to the spot. He stared at Sunil dumbfounded. As soon as Steve was out of earshot, he gripped Sunil by the shoulders.

'It's a total disaster,' Davey said, shaking him. His voice sounded full of fear. 'This is an emergency! I need Kaboom and I need it *now*!'

CHAPTER 13
BAT OR NO BAT

Davey and Sunil took off at breakneck speed down Eel Avenue to Kevin's place. They didn't have much time.

Kevin's dad answered the door. 'Kevin and George are still asleep, but feel free to wake them up,' he said with a grin.

George had slept over at Kevin's after staying up to watch Australia play India on TV. Kevin was snoring gently, his mouth hanging open. A thin trickle of drool had created a wet patch on his pillow. Sunil wanted to take a photo with his phone, but there was no time. George was curled up on a mattress on the floor.

'McNab!' Sunil shook his friend roughly. 'Pepi! Wake up!'

'What?' Kevin's eyes shot open in fright. He sat up and hastily wiped his mouth.

'Urgh!' George groaned as Davey nudged him with his foot.

'Davey needs help,' Sunil said. He grabbed some clothes from the floor and threw them at Kevin.

'Why?' Kevin asked as a pair of boxers hit him in the head. He pulled a face.

'I'm playing for the under-fourteens!'

'That's great!' George sat up.

'No it's not!' Sunil snapped. 'Have you seen how big they are? Davey's going to get eaten alive.'

'That's going a bit far,' Davey said drily.

'If we don't help him get back Kaboom, there could be nothing left of him by the time this game is over.' Sunil was pacing up and down the room.

Davey shot him a withering look. None of this was helping his confidence.

'You saw Mudge on Friday,' Kevin reminded them. 'He didn't let Kaboom out of his sight.'

'So,' Sunil concluded, 'wherever he is today, he'll have Kaboom with him!'

'Mudge plays lawn bowls at Penguin Palace RSL on Saturdays.' Kevin winked knowledgeably.

'We could go and plead with him,' Sunil suggested.

'He's not going to give us Kaboom!' Davey was running out of time. 'Mudge hates cricket even more than he hates me.'

George didn't say anything. He was deep in thought. 'We have to think more like Clouter,' he said finally.

Sunil made a face. '*Clouter*?'

'Mo didn't have Kaboom, but he offered us a trade and we took the bait,' George explained.

'Hook, line and sinker,' Davey muttered.

A car horn beeped outside.

'Thanks for trying, guys but it's no use.' Davey shrugged. 'I've got to go.'

'Wait!' Sunil grabbed his Kookaburra from his bag and handed it to his friend. 'You might need this.'

'Thanks, Deep.' Davey took the bat and left.

'Good luck!' his friends called after him.

Davey's stomach was in knots as they pulled up at the Shimmer Bay cricket ground. A large crowd of supporters had already gathered.

'Just in time,' Steve said. The umpires were already on the field.

They grabbed their gear and tumbled out of the car. Davey recognised a few people. His dad was sitting with a group of other fathers up in the stand. Howie gave Davey a wave.

'Go, Davey!' His dad gave him a big thumbs-up.

Davey waved back furiously and nearly whacked a Shimmer Bay player in the head with his elbow.

The player ducked just in time. 'Watch out!' he snapped.

Davey swung around to apologise and found himself face to face with Josh Jarrett, also known as Mr Perfect, the best cricket player Davey knew and the captain of the Sluggers' rivals, the Shimmer Bay Juniors.

'What are you doing here?' Davey asked.

'I could ask you the same question,' Josh said, looking amused. 'I sometimes sub for the Skiffs.'

'Guess I'll see you out there, then,' Davey said.

'This is the big league, Warner.' Josh smiled. 'Better keep your eyes open or you might get hurt.'

Davey wasn't sure which made him more nervous – seeing Josh, the game ahead, or having no Kaboom.

But he had no more time to worry about it. It was time to play cricket.

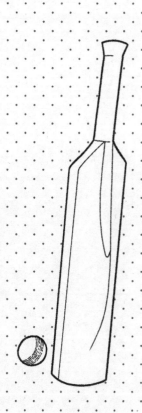

CHAPTER 14

THE BIG LEAGUE

The Shimmer Bay Skiffs won the toss and opted to bat first. Steve gathered the team together for a quick pep talk. Davey knew that, as captain, Steve would have to be on the go continuously, thinking on his feet and making it up as he went along. It was a huge job and now he had his little brother to look after.

'Today's a big match,' Steve said. 'Let's get out there and smash these guys, they're nothing.'

'Well, technically, their current for-and-against record against us is seven to one,' Jerome piped up. 'In their favour,' he added, a little unnecessarily.

'Yeah, but they don't play with heart like we do,' Steve countered with conviction.

'They've got seven rep players and the fastest bowler in the league,' Jerome pointed out.

'You can shut up now, Jerome.' Steve silenced his friend with a meaningful look.

Jerome shook his head, but stayed quiet.

'We've done the hard work,' Steve went on with enthusiasm. 'Just stay on form and do your best.'

The players nodded and wished each other a good game. Steve placed his fielders and saved Davey for last.

'You won't bowl today,' he told Davey. 'I'll get you to field at third slip.'

Davey nodded.

'You okay?' Steve asked.

Davey opened his mouth to reply, but no sound came out. He couldn't remember ever having felt this nervous.

'You can do it, Squirt,' Steve said. Then he added, 'Just don't mess up.'

As the opening batters approached the wickets, Davey took up his position.

His palms felt too wet and his mouth too dry. He stretched lightly on the spot, shifting his weight from one foot to the other, keeping his legs light and spry. It helped a little to have Steve's belief in him, but at the end of the day he was on his own.

Davey concentrated hard and tried to ignore the bowling ball in his stomach. He was going to do all he could to hold his own in the under-fourteens and, failing that, just stay alive.

The openers made a solid start, but off the fourth ball of the fifth over, Steve got one to duck away. The Skiffs' opening batter, Karesh, was drawn wide and his attempted drive only managed to get a thick edge. Davey flung himself to the right, stuck out his hand. He was as stunned as Karesh that he somehow managed to hold on to the edge. One wicket down.

'Not too shabby, bro!' Steve yelled. He ran over to give his brother a hug. Even Jerome gave Davey a nod of respect.

It was a start, but Shimmer Bay continued to bat well. Davey saw little action again until Josh came out as number four, at the fall of the next wicket. Davey was surprised that Josh batted so high in the order in this grade, and burned to get him out. Josh made a point of flashing Davey a big smile every time he scored a run – and that was too often. It was infuriating, but Davey grudgingly had to admit it – the guy could play.

Although he'd lost a couple of partners, Josh was batting really well and scoring quickly. With his own score on forty-six, he was shaping up to take the game away from them.

Then he edged one past the slips, down towards the third-man boundary. Davey

chased from third slip with everything he had and more. He thought he might throw up from the effort, but ran hard all the way. He picked the ball up just inside the boundary, turned and threw in one motion. The return was right over the stumps and Danny the wicketkeeper took the bails off. Josh had been looking to keep the strike, but didn't make his ground. He was run out!

'I kept my eyes open that time,' Davey said with a big smile when Josh passed him on his way off the field.

'Warner . . .' Josh muttered as he left. He looked furious.

The lower-order batters for the Skiffs kept the runs going and, at the end of their twenty-five overs, they were eight down for 128 – a challenging total.

It was the Saints' turn to bat, chasing 129 runs to win.

They lost two early wickets, but Steve went in at number four and their captain was in good form. He helped them reach sixty-five with only four wickets down. Davey tried not to get too excited. If they kept going at this rate, they should win.

But you never knew how quickly the tide could turn. The Skiffs' fast bowler, Zane, came back into the attack for a few overs and caused a collapse. The Saints lost four wickets for very few runs.

Davey was next in. He was batting at number ten. He picked up Sunil's bat. It wasn't Kaboom, but it was the closest thing he had.

'Go, Davey!' his dad shouted. Davey's stomach did another flip and he concentrated on taking deep breaths as he approached the pitch.

Steve was the other batter. The situation was dire. They had enough overs left, but still needed fifty-nine runs to win, with only two wickets standing.

'Try to give me all the strike and I'll get the runs,' Steve advised. 'You just have to stick around and grind this out.'

'I'll grind *you* out,' Davey said firmly. 'Put a sock in it, Steve.'

Steve glared at his young brother. 'I'm the captain and your job is just to defend,' he said.

They had a small chance of winning this game, if they didn't kill each other first.

The first ball Davey faced was a swinging yorker. He managed to jam his bat down on it and it squirted off to the leg side for one. Steve drove the next ball to the boundary for a four.

They pressed on. Little by little the target was reduced. Davey began to relax a little and started to time his shots better.

We can do this, Davey realised. *We could actually win!*

Although Zane peppered Davey with short and fast deliveries, he had made thirteen runs. *An unlucky number for* some, *but not me*, thought Davey.

Josh came on to bowl and over-pitched his first delivery. With a rush of confidence,

Davey instinctively knew what to do. He stepped down the wicket and drove the ball long and high over the bowler's head for four. The crowd loved it!

Josh glared at Davey.

'So much for getting hurt,' Davey said smugly.

Steve walked down the pitch and Davey thought he was coming to congratulate him on the shot. 'What was that?' his brother snapped.

'A great shot?' Davey felt on top of the world. 'A legend in my own lunchtime?'

'A loser who doesn't listen,' Steve hissed.

The two brothers glared at each other.

'Forget your history with Josh,' Steve said.
'I said *play it safe*! Protect your wicket, DO YOU
UNDERSTAND?'

Davey couldn't believe it. How dare Steve
bawl him out in front of everyone when he
was playing so well?

Who did Steve think he was? Davey
thought bitterly as Steve stalked back to his
end. He thought he could yell at Davey just
because he was his little brother. It was so
unfair!

Davey sneaked a look at the scoreboard
and the team watching from the sidelines.
They looked grim. He could just make out
Jerome and Danny glaring at him. With a
jolt, Davey realised Steve was right. He'd been
thinking about himself and not the whole
team.

Realising the seriousness of the situation, Davey concentrated on protecting his wicket while letting Steve score most of the runs. He deflected the next delivery off his hip for a single, to put Steve back on strike.

'Good one, Davey.' Steve praised his efforts.

The brothers communicated well and finally began to work together as a team. They managed to put on fifty runs together. While Davey's contribution was only seventeen, it was much needed. They were getting very close to the target.

With nine runs still needed to win, the Skiffs' best fast bowler, Zane, came back into the attack for his last over. Steve cut the first ball for four, but going for a big shot on the next ball, he was caught behind. That was it. He was out.

This time he didn't give Davey any advice as he walked off the pitch. Davey kind of wished he had.

The fate of the game rested with Davey and the Sandhill Saints' number eleven.

CHAPTER 15

POETRY IN MOTION

With just five runs still needed to win the game, out walked Harry, the number eleven batter. Harry was a great bowler but a well-known bunny. He'd do almost anything to get out of batting and the whole team supported him in this wish. It was harsh but true – Harry was the world's worst batter.

Davey met Harry mid-pitch. He noticed that Harry was carrying two bats.

'Your mates thought you might need this,' Harry said, handing a bat to Davey.

Davey took the bat and looked at it in surprise. It was Kaboom! Davey had never been so pleased to see a piece of wood in his life.

'What the . . . ?' Davey looked up at the stand and saw Kevin, George and Sunil with his dad. So the boys had made it to the game. And they'd brought Kaboom? Davey couldn't get his head around it. How did they get Kaboom away from Mudge?

'Forget about the bat, Davey,' Harry said. 'The team's stuck with an eleven-year-old and me. It's not looking pretty.'

'That's where you're wrong, Harry,' Davey said. He held Kaboom to his chest and felt a surge of confidence. 'This is a game changer. We can win this!'

'O-kay . . .' Harry looked doubtful. 'What's the plan?'

'We need five runs, right?'

Harry nodded. 'Yeah, I checked with the scorer.'

'Just try and block the first one somehow or let the ball hit you,' Davey said. 'No matter what happens, *run*. I'll be coming.'

'I'll do my best,' Harry said.

Harry moved back to his crease to face his first ball. He looked really nervous and Davey watched anxiously as Zane sent down one of

his fastest balls. Harry never had any hope of actually hitting the ball with his bat, but he bravely took it on the arm.

'Oof!' Harry grimaced as the ball made contact.

'Ooh,' cried the crowd in sympathy.

'Run!' Harry yelled, taking off from his end.

Davey took off and sprinted down the pitch with all his might. They just made it, scampering through for a leg bye.

Only four runs to go! Zane didn't look happy. He went back to the top of his mark and glared at Davey.

'This'll sort the men from the boys,' he said loudly enough for Davey to hear.

'If you thought that one hurt, wait till you feel this!'

Davey glanced at Harry, who was still rubbing his arm. He shut him out. Davey ignored Zane and his sledging and he thought about Ricky and everything he'd learned. He gripped Kaboom. All other distractions faded away. It was Davey, Kaboom and the ball.

'You'll feel it all right,' Davey said to himself, as his eyes followed Zane's every move.

Zane ran in and let fly a fast bouncer aimed straight at Davey's head.

'Ooh!' the Saints supporters voiced their alarm when they saw the trajectory of the ball.

Up until now Davey had tried to avoid hitting the short ball, ducking and weaving and concentrating on keeping his wicket. As the red blur came screaming towards him, Davey realised there would be no second chances. It was now or never. He had Kaboom back in his grip. He didn't even have to think about how to stand or hold his bat. It felt completely natural. It was time to take action.

'Show me what you've got, Kaboom,' Davey said. He kept his eyes fixed on the ball and swivelled on his left foot. Kaboom hooked the bouncer high and handsome, way over the fine leg boundary for a huge six!

They'd won! The crowd erupted in a roar and Davey felt completely stunned.

'We did it!' Harry yelled, running down the pitch towards him. He looked completely and utterly ecstatic.

It took a minute to sink in. They'd won. They'd won! Davey was suddenly surrounded by people jostling him, slapping him on the back.

As usual at the end of a game, the players from the two teams all shook hands with each other before leaving the field. Josh even managed a grudging 'Good shot, Warner', before joining his team to talk over their defeat.

Even Steve was beside himself. 'Well played, Davey,' he said, grabbing his brother in a bear hug. 'You little beauty!'

Rob, the selector, appeared at Davey's side, his little notebook in his hand. 'You played some impressive cricket today, Warner,' he said. 'I'll be keeping an eye on you.'

'Thanks!' Davey couldn't remember ever feeling so happy. He hugged Kaboom and ran to find his friends.

Later that night Sunil, George, Kevin and Davey were hoeing into homemade pizzas at Davey's house.

'I still don't understand how you got Mudge to give Kaboom back,' Davey said.

George chuckled. 'The poetry book. When we got sprung in the classroom, I stuck it in my pocket. I'd forgotten I still had it.'

'Urgh!' Davey pulled a face. 'Trundle and Mudge – so gross!' It was enough to turn him off his pizza. 'But what's that got to do with Kaboom?'

'I had to give Mudge something to keep him quiet. We sneaked into Penguin Palace RSL and found Mudge's bag. Sure enough, there was Kaboom. Remember he was taking it with him everywhere? So we took Kaboom, but we left Mudge his book.'

'So he'd know to keep quiet or we'd spill about his little crush!' Davey exclaimed. 'That's gold!'

George nodded smugly. 'I tell you one thing,' he said, before taking another bite of pizza and munching happily. 'I won't be doing rubbish pick-up for a long time!'

'Cheers to that!' Kevin agreed.

The friends clinked their glasses of lemonade. There was a day–night game of cricket on TV to watch and they had plenty to celebrate.

Just then they heard a loud cry from the kitchen.

'Max, you thieving mongrel!' A split second later, Max flew into the room past the boys with a whole salami gripped in his teeth. Max and Davey locked eyes for an instant before Max pinned his ears back and flattened himself under the couch.

'Have you seen Max?' Davey's mum appeared in the doorway, her apron covered in flour and pasta sauce. She was brandishing a wooden rolling pin.

George, Sunil and Kevin all looked at Davey.

'Sorry, Mum, he's not in here.'

'Hmm.' Davey's mum looked unconvinced, but after a quick glance around the room she stalked back to the kitchen. 'When I get my hands on that dog . . .'

Davey stuck his head under the couch. Max was gnawing enthusiastically on the sausage.

'Max, you're a mutt!' laughed Davey. 'But I'm glad someone else is in trouble with Mum for once!'

Keep It Down!

DAVID WARNER

with J.V. MCGEE, Illustrated by JULES FABER

SIMON & SCHUSTER
AUSTRALIA
A CBS COMPANY

FOR CANDICE

CONTENTS

CHAPTER 1

ELEVEN GREEN BATTERS . . .

'Warner, you're reserve keeper!' Sunil Deep was speaking in his team captain's voice, even though they were just having a hit in the playground before school.

'Aye, aye, cap'n.' Davey Warner bowed and doffed the old trucker's cap he called his baggy

green, but he wasn't exactly ecstatic as he trudged to the spot behind the wicket.

'It's not my thing,' he said to his friend, George Pepi, who was at the crease, bat in hand, waiting for Sunil to bowl. 'Batting – yep, definitely. A bit of spin bowling – if I'm needed. But wicket-keeping?' He shook his head.

Sunil ran in and bowled a fast ball on leg stump. George hit it off the front foot straight to mid-on. Ivy Mundine was there, and she quickly got her hands to the ball and threw it back. George didn't try for a run.

'Yeah, well, as soon as Dylan turns up you're free,' George said. He frowned. 'His mum must have forgotten to wake him up again.'

Dylan was often late. He told his friends it was his mum's fault, but Davey had noticed that Dylan's mum always seemed to be on time for parent–teacher interviews and when she had to see Mrs Trundle, the school principal, about Dylan breaking school rules again.

Still, nobody really minded. Dylan was one of those kids everyone liked – everyone except Mrs Trundle and their teacher, Mr Mudge.

With an invisible bat, Davey slogged an invisible ball for six. 'I wish he'd hurry up. I need a bit more time at the crease.' A real ball whizzed past his ear and George took the opportunity to run for a bye, bringing Kevin McNab, another of Davey's good friends, on to strike.

'What're you doing, Warner?' Sunil shouted. 'You're supposed to be keeping wicket, not pretending you're batting for Australia!'

Max, Davey's dog, was fielding at deep fine leg, even though Mrs Trundle had banned him from the school grounds for life. Now he chased the ball and, moments later, dropped it at Sunil's feet.

'I have to practise my shots for Friday,' Davey shouted. 'First game of the school comp. We've *got* to beat the Batfish!'

The last time Sandhill Flats Primary played Batfish Beach Primary they'd lost. Now they were thirsty for revenge.

Kevin nodded. 'Yep, gotta get those Batfish back.'

'You're a batfish!'

It was Mo Clouter, school bully and cricket detester. He and his friends Nero and Tony had wandered down to C playground to

look for something to do. They'd found it –
bothering the cricketers was one of their
favourite pastimes. Now they were standing
right behind Davey, talking loudly and
whistling, trying to put him off his game.

Davey tried to block them out. He focused
on Sunil, who let loose a fast bouncer down
the pitch.

Davey then Kevin ducked as the ball flew
over their heads and sailed past Mo and his
friends. 'Hey, watch what you're doing, Deep!'
Mo shouted.

Sunil gave them a friendly wave. 'Sorry!
Better get out of the way!'

But Mo didn't move. 'Hey, Shorty!' he called
to Davey. 'Guess you'll have to be wicket-keeper
from here on, now that Dylan's gone . . .'

Davey and Kevin glanced at each other.

'He's just late,' Davey shouted over his shoulder.

'Ha-ha!'

Davey turned around. Mo and his friends were holding their bellies and laughing like they'd just watched the funniest YouTube video ever.

Davey shook his head. 'What?'

'Yeah, three years late by the time you see him again. He's left. His whole family's gone. Didn't he tell you?'

Davey and the rest of the cricket team looked at each other. Dylan gone? Without telling them? He'd never do that.

'I don't believe it,' Davey said, turning his back on Mo and his crew.

'You'll find out soon enough!' Mo said. 'Right, guys?'

'Right!' Nero and Tony echoed.

'Dylan's gone, Shorty. His mum got some big job in a mine up north and they've moved. I heard Mrs Trundle tell Mudge last week.' Mo made a sad face. 'Guess he forgot to mention it to you.'

Mo and his fellow comedians lumbered off, laughing loudly.

Davey and the rest of the team stopped playing to discuss this latest piece of information.

'Do you reckon he's telling the truth?' George asked.

Sunil shrugged. 'Dunno. Dylan was off sick all last week. Maybe he was going to tell us then, but couldn't.'

Kevin stuck out his bottom lip. 'Hope it's not true. Who's gonna drive Mrs Trundle round the banana? Dylan's so-o-o-o good at that.'

They all nodded silently. Dylan had been an expert when it came to infuriating Mrs Trundle. He only had to step onto school grounds and wherever she was her eye would start twitching. It was fantastic to watch.

Davey felt a surge of fear rise in his stomach. If it *was* true – and it probably wasn't, because Mo was always making stuff up – Davey would miss Dylan, no doubt about it.

But, truth be told, that wasn't what Davey was most worried about. The surge of fear he felt was because, if Dylan *had* left, both the school team and the club cricket team would be without a wicket-keeper. Even worse, as reserve keeper, Davey would have to take on the job, at least until a substitute could be found. Which meant that at training he'd be spending too much time behind the wicket and less time at the crease. Worst of all, with the game coming up on Friday against Batfish Beach, Davey would most definitely have to keep wicket. Which he wasn't at all prepared for.

'Clouter's making it up,' Davey said. 'Dylan'll be here any minute.' But even though he tried to sound confident, the awful feeling didn't go away.

The school bell sounded. Max barked and tried to make a dash for it, but Davey caught him by the collar. 'You better get out of here before Trundle sees you,' he said, tugging the dog to the school gate.

Davey pushed Max through and surveyed the street. A few stragglers were still arriving to school, but there was no sign of Dylan.

Surely he wouldn't leave without saying goodbye, Davey thought. *And surely he wouldn't leave before the big match against the Batfish. Surely . . .*

CHAPTER 2
THE B4U FAN

Mr Mudge, the grumpiest teacher at Sandhill Flats Primary, stood in the doorway of the classroom and waved the students of 6M through. It was only 9.30 in the morning, but he already looked tired.

'Maybe Dylan's on the run?' Davey whispered loudly to Sunil as they squeezed past their teacher. Davey had recently seen a movie about a guy who'd been wrongly accused of something and everyone was after him. Maybe that had happened to Dylan, he thought, although he had to admit that when Dylan was accused of something he was usually guilty.

Sunil made a face. 'Yeah, well, Mrs Trundle's probably after him. But I don't think that's why he's not here.'

'If you're wondering where Dylan is, he's *moved*. Left on the weekend.' Mr Mudge sounded pleased.

Davey and Sunil looked at each other. So it was true. Dylan had gone. 'You'll have to be keeper, Warner. It's just the way it is,' Sunil whispered, before making his way to his seat in the far corner of the room.

Davey took his place near Bella Ferosi and Mo Clouter, in the opposite corner of the room from Sunil. Kevin and George occupied the other two corners. Mr Mudge's tactic of separating the four boys so they couldn't talk about cricket in class was certainly effective.

Mrs Trundle appeared in the doorway. Beside her was a tall girl with a long dark plait.

'Mrs Trundle!' Mr Mudge was grinning like a crocodile. 'Who do we have here?'

'Mr Mudge, 6M . . .' Mrs Trundle ushered the girl in. 'This is Tay Tui. She's new at our school. Tay doesn't know anyone here yet, so please introduce yourselves. I want everyone in Year Six to make her welcome.'

'I know Mo,' the new girl said in a clear voice. 'He's the cousin of my second-best friend, Shania.'

Mr Mudge smiled again. His ears, which changed colour to match his mood, were a rosy pink. 'Well, that's wonderful! Perhaps Mo can be your buddy for a while.' He looked across at the great galumph slumped in the chair beside Davey.

Mo nodded angelically. 'Sure, Sir. Shania's my favourite cousin.'

'In that case, Tay, we might sit you near Mo. He can help you settle in.'

Mr Mudge glanced at Bella Ferosi, school captain and 6M's most outstanding student. 'Bella, would you mind moving places? You can take Dylan's old spot.'

'I'd be happy to, Mr Mudge,' Bella said, smiling pleasantly and giving her ponytail a flick. In a split second, she'd packed up her belongings, dusted down the desk and moved to Dylan's place, right beside Kevin.

Davey looked at his friend with sympathy. Sitting next to Bella should have had its advantages, but Davey had never been able to copy any of her work because she always kept it well covered. She also always reported him to Mr Mudge for the tiniest things. Now it would be Kevin's turn.

As Mr Mudge showed Mrs Trundle out, Tay Tui wandered over to Davey's table. She pulled out the chair Bella had vacated, sat down and plonked her backpack on the desk.

Davey noticed Tay's bag had stuff written all over it, things like 'I♥B4U' and 'B4U4ME'.

Humming to herself, Tay unzipped her bag and took out her pencil case. It was covered in the same slogans.

The new girl was clearly a big fan of the boy band B4U, a band Davey and his friends couldn't stand on principle (the principle being that any band loved by so many girls must be bad).

Now Davey noticed that someone – probably Tay – had drawn portraits in blue pen of each of the B4U members on the pencil case. Davey tried to work out who was who, but the pictures didn't look much like Lochie, Wills, Finn and Zac, the four band members. (Davey kicked himself. *How do I even know their names?*)

Now he noticed that Tay was singing to herself. She wasn't too bad – but then he realised what she was singing. It was B4U's

big hit, the one that had catapulted the
band to the top of the charts, where
they'd been ever since, denying proper,
good bands a shot at fame. 'You're My One,
My Baby' was the worst song Davey had
ever heard. The trouble was, as soon as you
heard it you couldn't stop singing it – for
weeks. *Aargh*!

'Who said that?' Mudge peered around the
room with piggy eyes.

'Warner did, Sir.' It was Mo.

Davey woke from his awful daydream with
a start.

For once, Mr Mudge let it go through to
the keeper. He glared at Davey for a moment
before continuing. 'As I was saying, class, I'm
pleased to announce that one of 6M's students
has been selected to perform at the town hall

in the city as part of Senior Citizens' Week celebrations.'

Mr Mudge's lips parted, revealing a hint of yellow teeth. Davey guessed the teacher was attempting to smile kindly.

'As we all know, Kevin McNab is a ballroom dancer, which I must say is a far better use of your time' – Mudge looked across at Kevin and nodded approvingly – 'than playing cricket. Anyway, Kevin and his dance partner have been selected to perform with a troupe chosen from all over the city.'

Davey looked across at his friend and surreptitiously gave him the thumbs-up. Kevin rolled his eyes: he hated ballroom dancing, but his mum made him do it.

Mudge's ears glowed softly. 'So let's all give Kevin a clap and wish him luck for his performance this Friday. He should be very proud.'

6M burst into applause. But Davey sat there like a stunned toadfish. He looked across at Sunil, then Kevin, then George. They too were motionless, staring into space as if they'd been donged on the head by a fishmonger's mallet.

Davey was in such shock that even Tay Tui's singing couldn't stir him. Dylan's leaving had been bad enough. But now Kevin wouldn't be playing in the match on Friday either, and he was one of their best bats. How were Sandhill Flats going to even play against the Batfish, let alone *beat* them? It was too awful to contemplate.

And there was the new girl, Tay Tui, still singing, as if nothing was wrong.

'You know you need me, baby,
It's true, oo-oo-oo.'

Davey put his hands over his ears. *Aargh*!

'That was Warner again, Sir,' Mo said.

CHAPTER 3

NEW RECRUITS

Recess passed in a blur. At last the lunchtime bell rang. Finally, after a few false starts that caused Mr Mudge's ears to turn maroon, the teacher let the class out. Relieved, Davey grabbed his lunchbox and Kaboom, his special cricket bat made of English willow.

'At least we've got cricket training,' Davey said to his friends as they crossed the playground to their favourite lunch spot.

Sunil gave him a friendly push. 'Ready to get behind the wicket? I know you love it.'

Davey groaned. He turned to Kevin. 'McNab, didn't you realise the dancing thing was on the same day as the match?'

'No! I thought it wasn't on for ages.' Kevin shrugged. 'Mum didn't tell me. But don't worry, guys.' He sounded optimistic. 'I'll get her to write a letter to the dance people. I'll get out of it, no sweat.'

'You better.' George sounded glummer than Davey, if that was possible.

Kevin grinned. 'Leave it to me!'

'Ah, boys! Lovely to see you arrive to training on time!' It was the nice new teacher, Ms Maro.

'What's she doing here?' Davey whispered to Sunil.

Sunil gave a little shrug that only Davey saw. 'Hi, Ms Maro,' he said, smiling so his dimple showed. 'Are you helping out today?'

Ms Maro grinned like she'd been handed a huge piece of ice-cream cake. 'I'm the new coach, Sunil.' She looked around at the gathering team members. 'In case you haven't noticed, I *love* cricket! So when Mrs Trundle was looking for a coach for the school team, I put up my hand.' She clapped in excitement. 'We are going to have *so* much fun!'

Davey's heart lifted just a tiny bit. Even though Ms Maro came across as entirely loopy, she actually *was* fun most of the time.

'Well, in that case . . . As captain, I'd like to welcome you, Ms Maro,' Sunil said, putting out his hand. 'But I guess we better get to it. We've got a big game on Friday.'

Davey knew what his friend was up to: if there was one thing the cricket players hated it was standing around talking when they could be having a hit, even if they were two players down.

Ms Maro smiled sunnily. 'We'll get started as soon as I've made a couple of announcements,' she said firmly.

She motioned for everyone to move closer. 'Now, first, as you know, Dylan has moved schools, so we need a new wicket-keeper.'

A look of sorrow crossed her face but was gone as quickly as it had arrived. 'Secondly, as you probably also know, clever Kevin here is dancing for our senior citizens on Friday, so won't be able to play. That means we're two players short.'

'No, it's okay, Ms Maro,' Kevin called out. 'My mum's going to write a letter.'

Ms Maro reached into her pocket. 'She's already done it, Kevin,' she said, waving a piece of paper. 'Mums are always ahead of the game, eh?' She smiled. 'Now, your mum says here –' Ms Maro held up the letter '– that you won't be coming to school at all that day, because you have to catch a bus to the town hall in the city and be there two hours before the performance at one o'clock.'

She looked over at Kevin. 'So, while we're hitting sixes and catching out Batfish, you'll be spinning your partner round the dancefloor for the senior citizens!'

She tucked the letter back in her pocket. 'Kevin, we're proud of you, but we're going to miss you on Friday, aren't we team?'

'Yes, Ms Maro,' the cricketers said in monotone unison.

Davey gave Kevin a push. 'Good one, McNab!' he hissed. 'Now what do we do?'

'So what we're hoping to do is . . .' Ms Maro looked around excitedly, as if they were all about to embark on a trip to the moon. 'We're *hoping* to enlist a couple of *new* players.'

'Great idea, Miss,' Sunil said, smiling so his dimple showed. 'But no one else knows how to play. We've tried it before.'

Davey nodded in agreement. 'It's true, Miss,' he said.

'Well, I think our luck's about to change,' Ms Maro said. 'Because I happen to know of two people who are *very* keen to join the team.'

Suddenly, Davey became aware of a sound he'd hoped never to hear again, the sound of that awful B4U song.

Ms Maro gestured to someone behind him. 'Come on, guys, come forward so we can all meet you!'

The cricket team took a step back to clear a path, and the two new potential recruits made their way to the front.

Davey sucked in a breath. He heard George hiss 'Oh no!' and Kevin turned and glared at him in horror. Then Davey's eyes locked

on Sunil. The team captain was as pale as a freshly minted zombie.

'Has everyone met Tay Tui?' Ms Maro put her arm around the new girl's shoulder. 'Tay loves cricket and can't wait to try out for the team.'

The teacher's eyes sparkled. 'Of course, everyone knows our other candidate. He's better known for his skill on the footy field but he tells me he *loves* cricket as much! I wouldn't be surprised if he turns out to be the next Ricky Ponting!' Ms Maro put her arm around the other potential cricketer.

It was Mo.

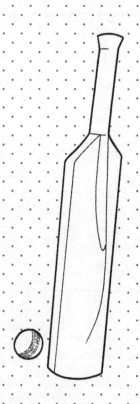

CHAPTER 4

KEEP IT DOWN!

Ms Maro wasted no time trying out Tay and Mo for the Sandhill Flats school cricket team.

Usually, the cricketers would have been glad to be out on the field playing, but this time their efforts looked half-hearted at

best. Not that anyone was too bothered about Tay Tui trying out. After all, she was nice enough and if she could play cricket, well, it'd be good to have her on board. No, nearly everyone seemed happy for Tay to try out – everyone except Davey, who had already heard enough of Tay's singing to last a lifetime. It wasn't really the singing he couldn't stand, but what she sang – that awful, stupid, mindless and gross 'You're My One, My Baby'. Really, who could listen to that song once, let alone 900 times?

Ivy Mundine seemed particularly pleased that another girl might join the team. But when it came to Mo, the cricketers would have voted as one, if they'd been asked: everyone would have been opposed.

It wasn't because they didn't like Mo, although nobody *did* like Mo, mainly because *he* didn't like anyone much, especially cricketers. It was because everyone knew, especially Davey, Sunil, George and Kevin, that Mo *hated* cricket more than anything else in the world. So the cricketers were asking: *Why?* And because Mo was always making things up and couldn't, as far as anyone could tell, be trusted, it was a triple: *Why? Why? Why?*

But Ms Maro appeared to be oblivious to the problem, which was why she'd promptly organised for the two potential recruits to show off their stuff.

Tay Tui, it turned out, had played wicket-keeper at her previous school. It was her favourite position, she said. So she donned the gloves and took her place behind the stumps.

'Davey, you bat!' Ms Maro called. 'George, can you bowl?'

The boys nodded and took their positions.

Ms Maro clapped her hands. 'Okay, guys, let's do it!'

George walked back to his mark, then turned and stopped for a moment, looking at Davey.

Davey eyed him back. He was standing at the crease, tapping his bat, Kaboom, on the pitch. But all he could hear was:

'You know you need me, baby,
It's true, oo-oo-oo.'

Tay was at it again, singing that stupid song. Davey couldn't think, let alone concentrate.

George ran in and bowled an inswinger. Davey, unable to get the dumb song out of his head, misjudged it. The ball caught the edge of Kaboom and whizzed behind him.

'Out!' For once, Tay had stopped singing. Davey looked around. She was holding the ball aloft in her glove. 'Out!' she called again.

Ms Maro clapped. 'Well done, Tay! That was fantastic!' She looked at Davey. 'Tay's pretty good, eh, Davey? But is she good enough for the Sandhill Flats school team?'

Davey looked at Ms Maro. She really was a nice teacher, and she did have lovely brown eyes, but sometimes he wished she was less . . . enthusiastic.

'Yeah, she's okay.' He turned and trudged off the pitch.

Ms Maro asked George to bowl a few more, this time to Kevin, but it was pretty obvious that Tay had made the team.

Soon it was Mo's turn. 'I'll bat,' he said grinning and waving a cricket bat around like a butterfly net.

'Deep, make sure you put him in it,' Davey said under his breath to his best friend. 'We're depending on you.'

'Thanks, Warner. Nice to be needed.' Sunil flashed him a half-smile and strolled out to his bowling mark looking determined.

Mo stood at the crease with his feet wide apart and stuck his bat out in the air in front of him. He bounced around on the spot. 'Send it down, Deep!' he hollered, baring his teeth. 'You can't beat me!'

Keep it down, Clouter! Davey thought. Mo had no idea how to hold a cricket bat.

Sunil bowled a yorker. Mo swung wildly, but missed by a metre or so. The ball sailed through to Tay, who caught it with one glove. In a second, she'd returned it to Sunil.

Sunil bowled again, this time an off-cutter.

Again Mo missed.

'Yeah!' Davey whispered. With a bit of luck, Mo might not make the team. He looked at George and Kevin. Simultaneously, they all held up crossed fingers.

Sunil bowled another attempted yorker. This time Mo ran down the pitch and managed to get an edge to the ball before it

bounced. Unfortunately, he hit it straight onto the bowler's wicket, sending the bails flying.

Ms Maro clapped her hands again. 'A good effort, Mo!' she called. 'Now, gather round, everyone, and let's have a chat.'

When everyone was in earshot, Ms Maro launched into her coach speech. 'I think we've got two new players with a lot of potential!' she said. 'Tay's our new wicket-keeper and Mo is first reserve. A bit more practice, Mo, and you'll soon be a key member of the team.'

She smiled so widely, Davey thought her face might crack. 'Congratulations, Tay and Mo! You're now officially members of the Sandhill Flats Primary School cricket team! Well done!' She clapped for the hundredth time that day.

The cricket team clapped too, but everyone appeared to be going through the motions. The thought of having Mo on the team was more than any sane cricketer could bear.

'Now, one more thing before we get back to training. This is serious . . .' Ms Maro suddenly looked so sad Davey felt like he should give her a hug.

'We've had a complaint . . . Someone – I don't know who – apparently said something unkind to the Batfish last time we played them.' Ms Maro glanced around. Davey thought her gaze lingered on him longer than the others.

'Now, as I'm sure you're all aware, at Sandhill Flats we play fairly, and putting the opposition off their game just isn't cricket.'

Ms Maro looked again at Davey, but he had no idea why. After all, Sunil was the one who had a way with words. Davey could never have even thought of half the things Sunil came up with. Like 'You smell like a fart in a firestorm' and 'Your sister chews cockroaches for fun'.

Ms Maro was still talking. 'The bottom line is, if any one of you says anything to put the Batfish off their game, we forfeit the match.' The teacher pursed her lips. 'Is that clear?'

Davey glanced at Sunil.

'Absolutely clear, Miss,' Sunil said. 'I don't know who was responsible last time, but it will never happen again while I'm captain.'

'Well, in that case, let's get to work!' Ms Maro handed a bat to Mo. 'Here you go.' She looked at Davey and smiled so her brown eyes sparkled. 'Davey, can you show Mo how to stand and give him a few tips?' She clapped her hands for the five-hundredth time that day. 'We're going to have so much fun! Watch out, Batfish!'

CHAPTER 5

A CRICKET CATASTROPHE

At lunchtime the next day, the Sandhill Flats school cricket team dawdled down to C playground for another training session.

Usually Davey and his friends looked forward to training so much they'd count

down the minutes. This time, however, they'd have preferred to be anywhere else.

For one thing, they missed Dylan. On the upside, they'd at least now heard from their friend, who had skyped George the night before and told him about his trip north, and how he'd seen the Big Banana and the Big Pineapple.

Also on the upside was the fact that everyone agreed Tay Tui might turn out to be an okay wicket-keeper – everyone, that is, except Davey, who still found Tay's singing and that stupid B4U song annoying.

But the boys were *extremely* disappointed that Kevin couldn't play on Friday against the Batfish, an unfortunate situation that had turned into a full-blown nightmare now Mo Clouter was in the team. Davey and his friends were unanimous about that – inviting Mo to join the team was like inviting a boa constrictor to a bandicoots' picnic. There could only be one outcome – and it wouldn't be pretty.

So, when they arrived at C playground to find Mo at the crease, swatting at balls like they were flies and yelling 'Not fair!' and 'You're toast!' every time he missed, Davey and his friends nearly turned around and trudged back to the classroom to spend the forty minutes with Mr Mudge. Anything had to be better than this.

At least Tay Tui was friendly, abandoning her post behind the wicket to offer everyone Whopper Chomp lollies from an open packet. 'I've never had these before!' she said, smiling widely. 'They're the best!'

Davey and his friends each took a sweet and nodded knowingly. Whopper Chomps were their favourite.

'Tay's all right,' Sunil said quietly in his captain's voice to Davey as he took the last sweet in the packet. 'She's in.'

Yeah, if she'd stop singing for a minute, Davey thought.

Ms Maro rushed over. 'Here you are!' she exclaimed joyfully, as if they were Santa's elves bearing gifts. 'Now, Davey, you can be the other batter. Sunil, you have a turn bowling. You other two can practise fielding in slips.'

Davey plodded to the bowler's end, dragging Kaboom behind him. He'd never felt so uninspired on a cricket pitch before.

Sunil paced out his run-up, then turned to face his nemesis. At least now Mo had his bat on the ground, but his feet were still wide apart, as if he was holding a golf club, and he was still bouncing on the spot.

Sunil ran in and bowled a full-length fast ball down the leg side. Mo ran out to meet it, trying to get his bat to it before it bounced. He missed and Tay Tui caught it and stumped him faster than Davey could say 'Ha!'

'Out!' Tay called.

'No' fair! Gi's another one! I'll smash it!' Mo was waving his bat threateningly in Sunil's direction.

Ms Maro stepped in. 'Okay, Mo, try again.' She turned to Sunil. 'Captain, we need to help our new recruit get up to speed. Bowl a little slower till Mo gets the hang of it.'

Sunil didn't smile or nod; in fact, Davey was sure he saw his best friend grimace before turning to go back to his mark.

Ms Maro glanced at her watch. 'Now guys, I have to pop down to the office for ten minutes. Keep it up and I'll be back before you can say "Six!"' She gave a tinkly laugh, then set off at a jog across the playground.

For once Sunil did as he was told, and bowled a slower ball. Mo managed to hit it and ran down the pitch. Davey ran too, but had to sidestep Mo, who had begun zigzagging in front of him.

'Move over, Shorty!' Mo laughed.

Now at the crease and waiting to bat, Davey tried to put Mo out of his mind, even though his batting partner was grinning like a pufferfish at the bowler's end.

He breathed deeply and tried to focus. *Eye on the ball. Eye on the ball . . .*

*'You're my one, my only, b-a-a-a-b-y-y-y,
   It's no fun, I'm so lonely, b-a-a-a-a-a-a-a-a-a-
b-b-b-b-y-y-y-y-y.'*

Tay was singing that stupid song again.

Aargh!

Sunil ran in and bowled a bouncer
down the leg side. Davey thought he'd try
his switch hit. He swapped the position
of his hands and turned. But his timing
was all wrong and in a split second the
ball was in Tay's gloves. Davey had to admit
she was pretty good.

'Close!' she said, flashing him a smile.

'She'll catch you next time!' Mo called from
the other end of the pitch.

Davey bit his tongue and gave him a friendly wave.

'If you care, if you care at all,
Just pick up your phone and make that
call . . .'

Davey turned. 'Hey Tay, keep it down!' he said in a friendly tone.

'What?' Tay looked confused. 'I didn't say anything.'

'You were singing.'

'Was I? Oh, sorry.' Tay shook her head as if she'd just woken from a deep sleep.

Davey tapped the pitch lightly with Kaboom and tried to focus again. *Take a deep breath. Eye on the ball . . .*

Sunil ran in. Just as he reached the bowler's crease, Mo hooted loudly.

The noise took Sunil by surprise, and his ball went wide.

Davey let it go through to Tay.

'Ha! Those Batfish are gonna win by a mile! Mo laughed.

'Clouter, you're on the team now,' Davey called out. 'You're one of *us*!'

Mo laughed again, and did a little shake and a wriggle. 'Maybe – or maybe not!'

Davey groaned.

'Shania said Mo was a bit thick.'

Davey turned.

Tay was grinning at him. 'But I kind of like him.'

Davey raised an eyebrow. 'That makes two – you and his mum.'

'He reminds me of Zac. You know, the tall one in B4U?' Tay stared into the middle distance, as if she'd been hypnotised. 'He's got those dark eyes.'

'Eeewwww!'

Tay shrugged and smiled to herself. *'You're my one –'*

'"MY ONLY BABY"! I *know!'* Davey had just about had enough. And it was only Tuesday.

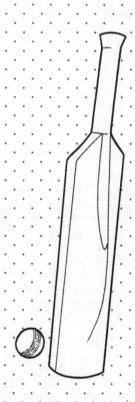

CHAPTER 6

CLEAN BOWLED
AND OUT

The big match against Batfish Beach Primary
was only two days away and things weren't
exactly going smoothly for the Sandhill Flats
team. Tay Tui had proved to be a more than
able wicket-keeper and replacement for Dylan,
but Mo Clouter was nothing short of a disaster
as a temporary fill-in for Kevin.

Everyone knew Mo hated cricket, so why he'd volunteered to join the school team was a mystery.

'He's up to something,' Davey said to Sunil as they dawdled into class on Wednesday morning.

'Yeah, and we need to find out what.'

'Deep, no more talk, unless it's about HSIE,' Mr Mudge barked.

Davey noticed that Mudge's ears already had a blood-orange tinge. However, the lesson started out reasonably well. Mudge droned on about the discovery of gold in Australia. Davey tried to listen – especially because George had said there was gold in the swamp at Flatter Park, and Davey thought Mr Mudge might get around to telling them how to find it. But soon the familiar sound of a certain

B4U song buzzed in his ear like a mosquito. Tay was at it again.

'... *pick up your phone and make that call* ...'

Davey tried to keep his eyes to the front. He figured that if he didn't look at Tay he'd have less chance of focusing on what she was singing. But it didn't work. For some reason, as soon as he heard the song he couldn't hear anything else.

He glanced in Tay's direction. She was in a trance again, staring into the middle distance as she sang. Davey noticed that on the desk in front of her was a Whopper Chomp packet.

Oh-oh, he thought. He'd seen this before. Mo Clouter had found a Whopper Chomp packet on his desk not so long ago and it had turned into a huge to-do because Sunil had hidden rotten egg gas in it. Mudge's ears had stayed purple for days.

'... *you're my on-ly, ba-a-a-a-b-b-b-y-y-y* ...'

Tay's hand reached absent-mindedly for the Whopper Chomp packet. She extracted a lolly and popped it in her mouth. The singing stopped.

But it was too late. 'Who's making that noise during HSIE?' Mudge's ears were tearing through the colours of the spectrum at the speed of sound. Davey couldn't take his eyes off them.

'Is that supposed to be singing? Whoever it is, don't think you're being funny.' The teacher looked around accusingly.

Mo put up his hand. 'It was Warner, Sir, singing that B4U song. He can't stop thinking about them.'

Mudge's cold gaze settled on Davey, his ears now violet.

Davey looked down at the desk in front of him. There, on top of his book, was Tay's Whopper Chomp packet. Someone – Mo – had pushed it there.

Mudge marched over and bent down so close that Davey could see bristles peeking out of his nostrils.

'Wa-a-a-a-r-ner!' Mr Mudge grabbed the lolly packet. 'What is this?'

'Not sure, Sir,' Davey mumbled. 'It's not mine.' He didn't say whose it was. He wasn't a snitch.

'They're Warner's, Sir.' It was Mo.

Mudge's ears had turned black. 'Is that correct, Warner?'

Davey looked at Tay Tui. She'd turned blue and her face had frozen in fear. He couldn't tell on her. 'Um, I don't know, Sir.'

'So while I'm out here doing my darnedest to fill that empty head of yours with at least a smidgeon of knowledge' – Mudge held up his thumb and forefinger to show how little knowledge he expected Davey to absorb – 'you're having a fine old time lazing around, singing songs and eating lollies. Is that right?'

'No, Mr Mudge.'

'Last time I found a packet of lollies on this table I recall that you were partly responsible.' Mudge turned to survey the class. 'And I promised you all then that if I *ever* found someone eating lollies again in class, I'd make an example of that person.'

'Yes, Mr Mudge.'

'Warner, I'm determined to teach you something, if it's the last thing I do.' Now Mudge's whole head was purple. It looked like a giant eggplant with hair. 'That's it. Instead of playing sport on Friday you can help me polish the lawn bowls. And if there's any time left over, I'm sure Mrs Trundle will be able to put you to good use.'

Mudge bared his teeth in an evil grin. 'So that means you'll miss the cricket match this week. You're going to have to learn the hard way.'

'Mr Mudge?' Tay had her hand up. 'I . . .'

Mudge shook his head sadly. 'Tay, no doubt you're feeling sorry for Warner, but he deserves everything he gets. He'll never learn, otherwise. So I don't want to hear any more about it.'

He peered around the room. 'I'm sure someone else could take Warner's place in Friday's game. Any volunteers?'

Bella Ferosi's hand shot up. 'I'm an excellent cricketer, Mr Mudge,' she said. 'I've never joined the cricket team because I'm the netball captain, as everyone knows.' She looked around the room, searching for confirmation. 'But we have a bye in netball this week, so I'd be happy to captain the cricket team.'

Grinning maliciously, Mudge looked across at Sunil. 'Well, I'll suggest that to Ms Maro,' he said. 'I'm sure she'd be happy to give you a turn as cricket captain, Bella. It's good to allow others the opportunity to shine, don't you agree, Deep?'

Davey eyed Sunil. His friend had that zombie look again. Sunil was proud to be captain of both the school team and their club team, the Sandhill Sluggers, and he had every right to be – he was a great captain, even if he did sometimes let slip the odd word or two to the other side.

Bella, on the other hand, was the bossiest person Davey had ever met. A cricket team with Bella and Mo in it was a team Davey would never want to join. He shook his head in despair.

'Don't worry, Shorty,' Mo whispered. 'I'll take care of those Batfish.' He giggled. 'You can count on me.'

CHAPTER 7
TRAINING TRAUMA

'Just because you can't play doesn't mean you can't come to training.' Sunil had his arm around Davey's shoulder as they rounded the toilet block and headed across C playground.

'Yeah, same as me,' Kevin said. 'I'm still going to training. It's better than sitting around doing nothing.'

They reached the cricket pitch. Some of the team were already there, but Ms Maro was yet to arrive.

'What about Bella?' Davey was in a funk. 'They can't make her captain!'

'Nah, that'll never happen.' Sunil sounded his usual happy self. 'I'll eat Mo's stinky hat if they make Bella captain.'

Davey was about to make Sunil shake on it – bets like these always cheered him up – when someone called out his name.

'Davey!'

He turned. Tay Tui was running towards them with Ivy Mundine close behind.

'I'm so sorry, bro!' Tay was panting. 'I tried to tell Mr Mudge again just now, but he still wouldn't listen. It was like he didn't really want to know . . .'

'He didn't. He's always like that.' Ivy frowned. 'It's bad luck, though. And now look who's coming.' She pointed.

They turned to see. Bella had just rounded the toilet block and was striding towards them. She was carrying a bat. When she saw them staring, she waved. 'Hi, everyone! You ready to get stuck in?'

'Don't tell me . . .' This time Sunil looked as if a vampire had drained his whole body of blood. Even the tips of his hair looked grey.

Bella paused to catch her breath, then put one hand on her hip. 'So, I'm thinking we'll start with some warm-ups, then we'll do ten laps of the playground. Then I'll practise my bowling while Tay and George bat. Sunil, you'll be wicket-keeper –'

'Um . . .'

Davey had never seen Sunil at a loss for words. There was always going to be a first time, though.

'Um . . . Um . . . Ah . . .'

'So, let's start with some stretches.' Bella dropped the bat she was holding. 'Everyone space out and do what I do.' She stood with her feet apart, took a deep breath and raised her arms.

No one moved. She stopped to look around.

Davey glanced at Sunil and stifled a laugh. The situation was so desperate it was funny. Sunil tried not to smile.

'Come on, guys! Let's get to it!' Bella reached up high then swung low, turning as she went, so her fingertips brushed her toes. She reversed the action. 'Now the other way. Davey? Sunil? Ivy?'

Still no one budged.

'Good to see you guys have started already! Well done!' Ms Maro was rushing towards them. The rest of the team were running behind, carrying the gear.

Bella turned. 'Ah, Ms Maro, you've made it at last.' She waited for the teacher and the other kids to reach them.

'Ms Maro, since I'm captain this week, I'd be happy to run the training. I'm a very good leader.' Bella smiled, then turned back to the cricketers, who now stood with their arms crossed.

'Thanks. That's a lovely offer.' Ms Maro smiled and patted the school captain on the back. 'But Sunil Deep is already team captain.'

'Mr Mudge said I could be!' Bella suddenly sounded like a four-year-old who'd been told Christmas was cancelled. 'He said it was time to give someone else an opportunity to shine – which I happen to be good at.' She gave her ponytail a flick. 'Shining, I mean.'

Ms Maro put her arm around Bella's shoulder, a look of sympathy on her face. 'Yes, I talked to Mr Mudge about that, and we agreed that perhaps this week was not the right week to change captain. If you'd like to join the team, that's great, but Sunil's our captain, isn't he, guys?'

'Yeah!' everyone shouted, punching the air in relief.

'No!' It was Mo. He'd sneaked up behind them.

'Mo, you've always got a funny line to keep us laughing!' Ms Maro shook her head in amusement. 'Now, let's get to it!'

Bella put her hands on her hips and frowned. 'I only joined on the condition that I be captain. I need to *lead*, Ms Maro, not *follow*.'

'Sorry, Bella,' Ms Maro said firmly. 'But I have to put the team first, and on this occasion that means keeping things as they are.'

Bella flicked her ponytail so hard Davey thought it might fly off. 'In that case, I'd better go. I have important duties to attend to.' With that, the school captain marched off across the playground.

'Looks like Bella won't be playing after all,' Sunil said quietly to Davey. 'Shame.'

'Yeah. Oh well . . .' Davey had to admit Ms Maro was a lot cleverer than she looked.

Ms Maro clapped her hands. 'So, let's get started.'

She looked over at Tay. The new girl had pulled a packet of Whopper Chomps out of her pocket and was about to extract a lolly from it. 'Tay, no lollies while we're training.'

Tay looked up in surprise. 'Sorry, Miss,' she said. She glanced at Ivy Mundine, who was standing right beside her. It seemed the two girls had become friends.

'*You're my one, my on-l-y-y-y-y-y* . . .' Tay sang.

'*B-a-a-a-b-y-y-y-y*,' Ivy sang in response. The girls burst out laughing.

Oh no, thought Davey. Now Tay had Ivy doing it. Where would it end?

Ms Maro frowned. 'Save your singing for choir, girls.' She turned to look at Davey. 'Mr Warner, I hear you won't be playing on Friday? That's a shame.'

'Yeah, Mr Mudge said I was singing in class and eating Whopper Chomps, Miss. But can I still train?'

'Of course, Davey.' Ms Maro glanced at Tay and Ivy. The two girls had finished their Whopper Chomps and singing and were busy setting up the wickets. 'And I might have a word to Mr Mudge.' She smiled. 'Now, Davey, grab Kaboom. You and George can bat first.'

Ms Maro wasn't half as kooky as she first appeared. In fact, Davey would have gone so far as to call her the best teacher he'd ever met. Not that she had much competition, now that he thought about it.

He ran over and grabbed Kaboom. He wasn't going to let anyone or anything stop him from playing the Batfish on Friday.

CHAPTER 8
TALKIN' TANGO

With Bella off to attend to her 'important duties' and Mo under Ms Maro's surveillance, training *should* have been fun. But despite repeated requests from the teacher, Tay continued to sing behind the wicket. She didn't even know she was doing it, Davey realised now, which made it all the more difficult to get her to stop. And once more it put Davey off his game.

And even though Ms Maro kept a close eye on Mo, the clueless cabbage still managed to wind up the entire team. One thing in particular that Mo said was so disturbing that Davey was forced to call an emergency after-school meeting of his three best friends.

He'd been standing at the crease, Kaboom in hand. Behind him, Mo was having a turn as wicket-keeper.

While Davey waited for George to bowl, and with Ms Maro well out of earshot, Mo kept up a constant stream of annoying talk. Most of it didn't even make any sense. But it was the next thing that Mo said that got Davey really worried. 'I'm gonna make sure those Batfish win on Friday, Shorty. Shouldn't be too hard.'

Davey turned around to eye Mo. There was never any point replying when Mo was fired up. And if he kept quiet, Mo would let slip what he was up to.

Mo went on, his chest puffing with pride. 'All I need to do is keep talking to their bowler on the field, let him know what I think of his style. And their fielders, and their wicket-keeper. That should do it.' Mo smirked like a sick toad. 'The Batfish'll thank me after.'

So as soon as training had finished, Davey called the meeting for after school. For convenience, it was held at the corner shop, which belonged to Benny, the Sandhill Sluggers' coach, and his wife, Barb.

'So what's all this about, Warner?' Sunil looked serious.

'Clouter's planning to put the Batfish off their play so we forfeit the game.'

'How do you know?' Kevin looked sceptical.

'He told me. He's going to say things to them when they're fielding.'

'Well, that's it,' Sunil said firmly. 'We've got to get him out of the team.'

'And while we're at it, can we do something about Tay Tui?' Davey knew Tay was good behind the wicket, but something had to be done.

'What do you mean?' Sunil looked confused. 'She's pretty good. And she likes Whopper Chomps, which is handy.'

'Yeah, but she sings all day. That horrible B4U song. It's driving me mad!'

The other three boys shook their heads. 'Yeah, that song really sucks,' George said.

'It's a shocker.' Kevin sighed.

'Sure is.' Sunil looked thoughtful for a moment. He snapped his fingers. 'Got it! Tay can't sing if she's sucking a Whopper Chomp. So we load her up with them every time we play.' He looked around at his friends. 'We'll have to pool our money for this. Do it for the team, okay?'

They all nodded. It was such a simple but clever plan. Sunil really was a genius, Davey decided.

'But what about Clouter?' Davey knew this wasn't going to be an easy one.

Sunil snapped his fingers again. 'Easy! We send him to another cricket ground. We'll just tell him it's over at Shimmer Bay Park. By the time he finds out, we'll have finished the game.' Sunil smiled and tapped his head.

'Mmmm, not sure,' Kevin said.

'Why?' George asked. 'Sounds like a good plan to me.'

'No, it won't work,' Davey said. 'Ms Maro's already told us it's a home Batfish game, so Clouter will smell a rat if we tell him it's changed.'

Sunil's smile faded. He shrugged. 'Yeah, maybe you're right. But we've got to do something. In the meantime, everyone needs to put in money so we can buy a shedload of Whopper Chomps for Tay. Now!'

The boys all made a show of emptying their pockets. Sunil waited, his arms folded, until they'd coughed up everything they had. Then he added it all up on the counter.

Benny watched from behind his newspaper. 'You boys having a party?' he said when Sunil pushed the pile of coins towards him.

'Nah, someone else will be, though. Give us six packs of Whopper Chomps please, Benny. That should do it.'

Davey watched as the money changed hands and Sunil pocketed the lolly packets. 'Don't go sampling them, Deep,' he said. 'We're going to need every single one of those.'

Sunil smiled so his dimple showed. 'You can trust me. Now, what about Clouter?'

'We could tell Ms Maro what he said.'
George looked uncertain. It wasn't a solution
any of them would usually consider. 'Never
tell, never worry,' was their motto.

The other boys shook their heads. Even
though Mo was a pugnacious pest, they
wouldn't go so far as to tell on him.

'No point dragging in teachers. Takes all
the fun out of it.' Sunil grimaced.

'I think we just have to make sure McNab
and Warner play,' George said. 'Clouter's
only a reserve. So if they can play, he'll have
to sit out.'

'But couldn't he call out from the sidelines?'
Now Kevin was doing the thinking.

Davey shook his head. 'He'll be sitting next
to Ms Maro. He won't be able to.'

Sunil looked around at his friends. 'So tonight, we all need to come up with a plan to make sure McNab gets out of the dance thing and Mudge lets Warner play. How hard can it be?'

Everyone shook hands. But later, as Davey rode home on his old bike, with Max trotting along beside him, he couldn't help thinking it could be very hard indeed. Kevin's mum was dead keen on him dancing, and she was no pushover. And as for Mr Mudge . . .

CHAPTER 9

MARO MAGIC

Davey left for school early the next day.
As soon as he arrived, he headed for
Ms Maro's classroom, where she could be
found most mornings, getting things ready
for the first lesson. He knocked on the
open door.

Ms Maro was at her desk, marking work. She looked up and smiled. 'Mr Warner! What brings you here?'

Davey took a few tentative steps into the classroom. 'I – I – I was wondering whether you ended up talking to Mr Mudge.'

The teacher put her head on one side and raised her eyebrows in question.

'About whether I can play against the Batfish tomorrow,' Davey explained. 'You see, I wasn't singing or eating lollies in class. It wasn't me.'

'Ah!' Ms Maro nodded knowingly. 'I'm sure it wasn't. I haven't spoken to Mr Mudge yet, but I will, right now.'

She got to her feet and smiled as if she'd just seen a rainbow. 'Mr Mudge isn't really mean,

you know, Davey. I'm sure I can talk him around.'

I'm sure you can, Davey thought. Somehow, Ms Maro seemed to always get her way. If anyone could help him get back in the team for Friday's game against the Batfish, it was her.

With his mission accomplished, Davey headed down to C playground, where Sunil and the others were already playing cricket. Tay was behind the wicket, Sunil was at the crease and George was bowling. Ivy was also at the bowler's end, bat in hand.

George bowled. Sunil moved forward down the pitch but his bat didn't connect with the ball. A split second later, Tay had stumped him.

'Out, Deep!' Davey yelled.

Sunil stopped in his tracks, turned and gave the new wicket-keeper a little clap. 'You're good, Tui, really good,' he said, nodding. He looked over at Davey. 'Warner, you have a turn. But watch out for Tay!'

Davey pulled Kaboom out of his backpack. He wandered over and took his position at the crease. *Here we go*, he thought. *She'll start singing that awful song any minute.*

But there was silence. Davey glanced behind him. Tay was in position, but her cheeks were bulging like a bullfrog's.

'How's it going?' Davey said as a test.

Tay nodded and made a loud sucking noise.

Davey smiled. 'So you like those Whopper Chomps?'

Tay nodded again and gave him the thumbs-up. She grinned. Her mouth was chock-full of lollies.

She wouldn't be doing any singing for a while, Davey decided. It solved that problem, at least temporarily. Now Davey and his friends had to work on making sure he and Kevin played in Friday's match.

'Ready, Warner?' George was standing at his mark, waiting to bowl.

Davey tapped Kaboom on the ground. 'You bet!'

For the first time all week, Davey got to bat in peace, and managed to pull off some nice shots. But soon the school bell sounded and the cricketers had to pull up stumps.

'So, any ideas about how we can get Warner and McNab back in the team for tomorrow?' Sunil asked as they strolled across the playground to class.

'Yeah, I know what I'm going to do.' Davey glanced at his friend – he knew Sunil wouldn't like his plan.

'What?'

'I'm going to beg for mercy,' Davey said. 'I've already asked Ms Maro to put in a good word for me. Now I'm going to offer to polish Mudge's lawn bowls and help out Mrs Trundle.'

Sunil frowned. 'That's a lame idea, Warner. Not very imaginative.'

'Maybe, but it's all I could come up with.'

Sunil looked disappointed. 'Okay, give it a try.' He glanced around at the others. 'What about McNab? Any thoughts?'

'I've got a few.' George looked confident. 'Kevin could let off the fire alarm at the town hall so they have to evacuate.'

Sunil shook his head. 'But he wouldn't get back quickly enough.'

'I could sneak off early, before we leave to catch the bus, and then turn up to the match in disguise.' Judging from his face, even Kevin knew it wouldn't work.

Sunil looked unimpressed. 'Next!'

'Okay, I've got one.' George sounded confident.

'Yeah? What?' Everyone was all ears.

George was about to explain when they rounded the corner of the toilet block and bumped into Mr Mudge.

'Warner, Ms Maro tells me you've offered to do a few jobs around the school today in return for permission to play in the match against Batfish Beach tomorrow.' Judging by the colour of his ears, for once the teacher wasn't irate.

Davey nodded. 'Yes, Sir. Anything you like.'

George and Kevin gave him a pat on the back.

'Excellent.' Mr Mudge crossed his arms. 'So, at recess, you can polish the lawn bowls. At lunch, report to Mrs Trundle. There are quite a few things that need doing around her office. I'm sure she'll find a use for you.'

'No problem, Mr Mudge.'

Mr Mudge waved them past. 'Now, straight to class.'

They set off again, moving quickly this time, with Mudge bringing up the rear.

'Good one, Warner,' Sunil whispered in Davey's ear as they approached the classroom. 'What a crazy idea! Who'd have thought you'd pull it off?'

Davey rolled his eyes. 'Thanks for the vote of confidence, Deep.'

'Now, we've just got to get McNab out of his dancing thing,' Sunil muttered. 'Wonder what Pepi's other idea was?'

CHAPTER 10

GEORGE'S
NO-BRAINER

Davey spent all of recess in the sports
storeroom polishing the school's lawn bowls.

Mr Mudge, who loved lawn bowls
almost as much as he hated cricket, was on
hand to supervise. 'Like this, Warner,' he
said, carefully picking up one of the bowls as

if it was a brand-new puppy. He dipped a rag into a bucket of warm soapy water. 'Gently rub it in circles. Then use another rag to dry.'

For once, Davey made a real effort to do exactly what his teacher asked.

'Once it's dry, you give it a quick spray with the polish, and then another good rub until it shines. Got it?'

Davey nodded and eyed the six sets of bowls that Mr Mudge had lined up. It would take all recess and lunchtime to get it done.

Mr Mudge seemed to read his mind. 'These will keep you busy for a while. So you'll have to help Mrs Trundle *after* school.'

Davey nodded. Whatever Mrs Trundle had lined up for him, he figured it would be worth

it if it meant he could play in the match the next day.

But at the end of the school day, when he was standing in Mrs Trundle's office, his optimism evaporated.

'I have just the job for a boy like you.' Mrs Trundle's eye twitched as she led him towards the big cupboard in the corner.

She pulled open the cupboard doors to reveal the shelves within. They were stacked with all kinds of stationery – scissors and glue, rulers and erasers, protractors and pins, boxes of bulldog clips.

The centre shelves were stacked closely together. Now Mrs Trundle pulled one of them towards her, like a drawer. Davey leaned forward to see what was on it.

Paperclips. Thousands of them, all in little compartments.

Davey had heard the legend of Mrs Trundle's paperclip collection, but no one had ever actually seen it so Davey had never believed the stories were true. And yet here he was, staring at the collection, perhaps the first person in the world (other than Mrs Trundle) to ever set eyes on it.

'It's the biggest paperclip collection in the southern hemisphere,' Mrs Trundle said proudly. There are four shelves like this one. But, as you can see, they need some re-sorting. That's your job.'

Davey took a closer look. Even he had to admit that the paperclips were in some disarray, with big ones jumbled in with small ones, and blue ones with orange ones.

Mrs Trundle glanced up at the big clock on the wall. 'I'll be here until half past five. You have until then to get these in order.' She smiled. 'You might receive a merit award for this, David. Now, chop chop!'

By the time Davey climbed on his bike to ride home, he could hardly see from all the sizing and sorting and picking and positioning. When he reached his house, Sunil, George and Kevin were hitting a ball around on the footpath out the front.

Sunil stopped in the middle of his bowling run-up. 'How'd you go?'

'Done! I'm in!' Davey raised his fist in victory. 'Batfish, here I come!'

'Good one!' Sunil gave him a slap on the back.

George put his hand in his pocket and pulled out a Whopper Chomp. 'Here, Warner, a little reward.'

Davey popped the lolly into his mouth.

'We've got some other good news,' Sunil said. 'Pepi has come up with a good plan to get McNab out of dancing.'

'Yeah? What?'

'Well, I've been reading about tarantulas,' George said. 'Apparently, if one bites you it makes you dance like crazy and wave your arms about.'

'Mmm. And?' Davey couldn't see what any of this had to do with Kevin, but he was keen to find out.

'So the idea is, Kevin pretends he's been bitten by a tarantula and does a crazy dance, waving his arms around a lot. He won't be able to do the ballroom dancing because you have to hold your partner the whole time.'

Davey made a cross-eyed face. 'Doesn't that mean he'll miss the cricket too?'

'No. He just does it long enough to miss going to the dancing thing, and then gets better in time to play cricket. It's brilliant!' Sunil's eyes were shining with excitement.

'Wouldn't it be easier to pretend to be sick?' Davey asked.

'Nah, Mum won't fall for that,' Kevin said. 'But spiders! She hates them, so it'll freak her out. And Dad's away, so he won't know.'

'Of course, there aren't actually any tarantulas in Australia,' Sunil said knowledgeably. 'And it's true that a tarantula bite doesn't actually make you dance so much as twitch – and only *sometimes*. But, you've got to admit, it's brilliant, a no-brainer. Much better than yours, Warner.' Sunil grinned.

'Yeah, it's good,' Davey said. 'Do you need a big spider? Because I know where one lives. I might be able to catch it, so long as you don't hurt it.'

Kevin put his hand on his heart. 'Promise.'

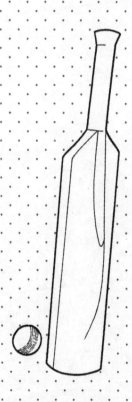

CHAPTER 11
'TARANTULA'

That night after dinner, Davey passed up a game of backyard cricket with his brother, Steve. 'Nah, I'm too tired,' he said, rubbing his eyes.

Davey's mum looked at him as if he'd turned into an alien. 'You? Tired? What've you been up to?'

'Nothing . . . But I need a jar with a lid. There's a spider on my wall and I need to catch him to put him outside.'

After a lot of rattling around in the back of a cupboard, Davey's mum found an old Vegemite jar. 'Careful not to drop it,' she said. 'And make sure you let him out as far away as possible. *I hate spiders.*'

Armed with the jar and broom, Davey and his dog Max headed for Davey's bedroom. The spider Davey was after often hid behind the poster of Ricky Ponting that hung on his bedroom wall.

After punching a few holes in the jar lid with a pen nib, Davey climbed onto his bed and carefully tugged on the corner of the poster. 'Whoops,' he whispered. The sticky stuff on the back of the corner had come off the wall, bringing a big chunk of

paint with it. 'Don't tell Mum,' he hissed
at Max.

Davey peered behind the poster, but it
was too dark to see. 'Max, get the torch!'
He pointed at the bedside table.

Max wagged his tail and barked before
dashing out through the door. Davey heard the
sound of his claws skittering down the hallway.

'Idiot pooch,' he muttered as he reached
down and grabbed the penlight. He switched
it on and shone it up behind Ricky. In the
upper corner, he spotted a dark shadowy
form. 'Gotcha!'

Except he hadn't, not yet. He grabbed the
broom and gently poked the end up behind
the poster. Nothing happened. He shone
the light up again – the spidery form hadn't
moved.

Max ran in and barked.

'We'll have to take Ricky down.' Davey
gently pulled the other bottom corner of the
poster off the wall. 'Ouch.' Another big chunk
of wall and paint came off. He reached up
and tugged carefully at a top corner – the
one he was fairly sure didn't hide a giant
spider. He looked down at Max, who was
standing on the bed next to him, his two
front paws up on the wall.

'Ready?' With the jar in one hand and
the broom in the other, Davey pulled on
the last corner. At the same time the poster
came away, a big brown spider scuttled down
the wall. Davey quickly stuck the broom in
front of it. The spider clambered on and in
a moment was running down the handle
towards him. Still holding the broom, Davey
held the jar at the end of handle. The spider
ran straight into it.

'The lid!' Davey slapped his hand over the top of the jar and cast his eyes around. There it was near the end of his bed. He dived and slammed it on.

'*Now* I've gotcha!'

After setting the jar on his bedside table, Davey rescued his poster of Ricky Ponting and stuck it up quickly, so his mum wouldn't see all the chunks out of the wall.

'So, what do you reckon, Ricky?' Davey stared into the former Australian captain's eyes. 'Will things work out tomorrow?'

Ricky's face looked like a huge green moon in the half-light of dusk. Davey threw himself back on the bed, and Max jumped on top of him.

'Get off!' Davey pushed the dog to the floor.

It had been a long day of polishing lawn bowls, sorting paperclips and catching spiders. Davey could hardly keep his eyes open. Still, he stared up at Ricky. 'Can we beat the Batfish, Ricky?' he whispered.

Did he see his hero wink? A thought came into his mind out of nowhere. Tay Tui was a good wicket-keeper – a *really* good one. If she also liked to sing, well, he'd have to get used to that.

But what about Mo?!

Davey knew what his mum would say. *'Give him a chance! Maybe Mo will learn to love cricket.'*

'Hmmm.' Davey wasn't buying it. That was *never* going to happen.

He looked at his spider. 'We're counting on you,' he said.

The creature was playing dead, but Davey was sure he saw one of its legs move . . .

The next morning, Davey was up early. After a quick breakfast of Corn Pops, he grabbed everything needed for the big game and jumped on his bike.

Stuffed into his school backpack he had his cricket gear, his bat, Kaboom, his 'baggy green', and, importantly, the Vegemite jar with the spider in it.

'Max, you're staying here,' he said firmly as he closed the back door behind him. Davey's dog was not only banned from the school grounds but from any school sporting fixture in the district. Max was that famous.

Davey wheeled his bike down the side path, then jumped on and headed to Kevin's place to give him the spider.

He couldn't let his friend down. After all, it was going to be incredible. He could see his friend now, doing the tarantula dance and freaking out his mum.

Davey laughed out loud. Mrs McNab would fall for it for sure. He could feel it in his bones.

CHAPTER 12

SANDHILL FLATS SLUMP

Lessons dragged that Friday morning. Mr Mudge seemed to take forever to explain long division for the hundredth time. Then he droned on about healthy eating choices in PDHPE for an hour, before asking Bella Ferosi to make an impromptu speech about leadership. Finally, after what

felt like thirty-seven hours, 6M was allowed out for lunch.

Davey, Sunil and George quickly made their way to the school gate to wait for the rest of the cricket team. The plan was to walk to Flatter Park around the corner, where the match would be played.

'No sign of McNab,' George observed as they strode towards the gate and freedom.

'We'll see him down at Flatter.' Sunil seemed confident. 'He's got to be sick and crazy enough to miss the dancing but get better quickly enough to make the match. It's a fine line, but I reckon he'll do it.'

Davey wanted to believe his friend, but now he wasn't so sure. For one thing, the spider had played dead for so long he wondered whether it was actually alive at all. In which case, would Kevin's mum fall for the trick? It was touch and go.

At the gate, Ms Maro was ticking names off a list. 'Ah, here they are! My star players!' She smiled at Davey and his friends, then looked up and over their heads. 'Oh, and here's Mo and Tay and Ivy! I didn't hear you coming!'

Davey glanced around. Tay, Ivy and Mo were a few steps behind them. But Ms Maro was right: the girls' mouths were so full of lollies, they couldn't make a sound.

'Hi, everyone!' Mo leered at Davey. 'Looking forward to losing?'

Davey gave the mini-minded muppet a happy smile.

When everyone was accounted for, the team formed two straggly lines and set off towards Flatter Park.

Two and a half minutes later, they were there. The Batfish Beach team had already arrived and had started warming up.

Davey scanned the field. Kevin was nowhere to be seen. 'McNab's not here,' he said quietly to Sunil.

'That's okay. If he comes any time before afternoon tea, they'll let him play.' Sunil still sounded confident.

'So long as Mo doesn't say anything to the Batfish before McNab gets here.'

'It's a risk we'll have to take.'

When it was time to toss the coin, Kevin still hadn't arrived. Sunil called tails, won, and opted to bat first.

'Hopefully McNab makes it by the time it's his turn to bat,' Sunil whispered as Davey pulled on his helmet and gloves. Then he'll be here to do some bowling when the Batfish are in.'

As he trudged out to the pitch with George, who was Sandhill Flats' other opening batsman, Davey scanned Flatter Drive. Still no sign of Kevin.

He took his place at the crease and tried to put Kevin, Mo and that awful B4U song out of his head for good. At this point, his main job was to take his time, score some runs and set Sandhill Flats up for a nice big run tally. He gave Kaboom a quick kiss for good luck. 'Come on, K, we can do this,' he whispered to his bat. Then he got into position and waited, ready.

The first Batfish bowler started with a few leg-spinners. Davey took it slow – so slow that by the end of the over he hadn't scored a run.

That's okay, he told himself. No rush. Then George at the other end also played out a maiden over.

After two overs with no runs to the score, Davey was pleased when, first ball next over, the bowler strayed down the leg side. Davey shifted his weight onto his back foot and pulled the ball to cow corner for three.

With George on strike, Davey watched as his friend blocked the first few balls. George was right to take it slow, he knew; but he was out LBW to the last ball of the over. He hadn't even had a chance to settle in.

Davey grimaced as George trudged off. One for three was not a great start.

Next up was Ivy. As she approached, Davey noticed she was no longer sucking on a lolly. He just hoped she wasn't going to start singing, like her new friend Tay.

But Ivy didn't sing – at least, Davey couldn't hear her. Instead she started scoring steadily with some stylish shots that had the Batfish fielders running everywhere.

It gave Davey the confidence to try a couple of his own scoring shots and forget about Kevin, Mo and B4U in the process. His score climbed to fourteen.

When Byron, the Batfish captain, sent a fast one down the leg side, Davey jumped at the chance to try his switch hit, something he'd been working on for ages.

With some fancy footwork, he turned, swapped hands on the bat handle, and played a right-handed drive for four valuable runs.

'Now we're getting somewhere!' Ivy called out from the other end of the pitch.

But a few balls later, Davey was out for twenty-one, caught in slips when Kaboom didn't quite connect.

Usually at this point, Kevin would have come in to bat. But as Davey traipsed back to the boundary his friend was still nowhere to be seen.

'Good one, Shorty,' Mo hissed as Davey passed. 'Wait till I get out there and start bothering those Batfish. Ha!' Mo's pink eyes were gleaming.

Ignoring the blithering blockhead, Davey eyed Sunil. 'No McNab?'

Sunil shook his head. 'Not yet. Tay's up instead.'

'Tay, no lollies out there,' Ms Maro said as the new girl pulled on her gloves. 'We don't want you to choke.'

'Sure, Miss,' Tay said before heading out to the pitch. 'I don't have any left, anyway.'

That's a worry, Davey thought. *Tay'll be singing for the rest of the match.* He made a note to ask to field on the boundary, as far as possible from the warbling wicket-keeper.

Davey had no idea whether Tay or Ivy were singing out on the pitch. But they certainly made some great shots and scored some quick

runs. When Tay did get out it was unlucky –
she stumbled going for a quick single and was
run out. Still, she had scored a respectable
sixteen runs.

Even without Kevin playing, it now looked
as if they'd reach a competitive total, but when
Ivy was dismissed for nineteen, it led to a
collapse. The rest of the Sandhill Flats batters
came and went with almost no runs added
to the score. Sunil, at his usual number ten
position in the batting order, added a few runs
to the tally before being caught behind.

The result was that, even though Ivy, Tay
and Davey had batted well and notched up
decent scores, Davey doubted it would be
enough. To have any chance of beating the
Batfish, Sandhill Flats would need at least
eighty-five runs or so. As it was, they were
sitting on sixty-nine. It would be up to their
last batter to bump up the score.

Unfortunately, with no sign of Kevin, the only batter left for Sandhill Flats was Mo Clouter.

Davey, George and Sunil exchanged worried looks. If Mo's performance at cricket training was anything to go by, his chances of scoring even one run were slim. On top of that, the cocky cabbage was no doubt hell-bent on pestering the Batfish. If that happened and he was caught, Sandhill Flats would be disqualified on the spot.

They watched as Mo grabbed a bat and started swatting invisible flies before tramping across the field towards the crease.

George shook his head. 'How did it come to this? I was sure our spider plan would work.'

'Yeah, me too,' Sunil said. 'It seemed like a no-brainer.'

Davey nodded. 'It did. Speaking of no-brainers, Mo's almost ready to go.'

They held their breath . . .

CHAPTER 13

THE WARBLING WICKET-KEEPER

Davey watched as Mo planted his feet wide apart and waved his bat around in the air. 'Keep the bat *down*! Didn't he learn anything at training?'

'Not about cricket,' George said.

The bowler ran in and let the ball fly.

Mo ran forward, holding his bat as if he was playing ping pong. He swung at the ball, which sailed past him and straight into the wicket-keeper's gloves. Mo was halfway down the pitch as the wicket-keeper casually stumped him.

He was out for a golden duck.

The Batfish jumped for joy.

Mo turned and looked behind him, then threw his bat on the ground and stormed off.

Davey sighed loudly. 'Well, that's it, then. All out for sixty-nine. We're done like a dinner.'

'At least he didn't get a chance to say much out there,' Sunil said.

'He couldn't have anyway,' George said. 'Check him out.'

Now only metres away, they could see that his cheeks were bulging so much he really did look like a pufferfish.

'Whopper Chomps,' Sunil whispered.

'You're my one, my only-y-y-y-y –'

Davey turned. Tay was back at it. He groaned.

Ms Maro clapped her hands. 'Tay, quiet for a moment, please.' She smiled. 'Now, everyone, gather round.'

The players dragged themselves to their feet and formed a ragged circle around the teacher.

'You all did a great job out there,' Ms Maro said as she offered around the oranges. 'Ivy, Tay and Davey, in particular, were wonderful!' Ms Maro's brown eyes sparkled as if she'd just seen a fairy at the bottom of the garden. 'Now we need to stay focused, and remember all those things we've been practising around catching and throwing.'

'Yes, Ms Maro.' The team tried to sound enthusiastic, but everyone knew they'd need a miracle to save this one.

'Now, Sunil, how do you want to set the field?' Ms Maro handed the captain the shiny new ball.

Davey jumped in. 'Can I go deep cover?' he said, wiggling his eyebrows at Sunil. Now that Tay was out of Whopper Chomps, he most definitely wanted to be well out of range of her singing.

Sunil nodded and winked. 'Sure. And Clouter, you're at deep fine leg – over there.' Sunil pointed.

Davey figured his friend was hoping to keep Mo out of earshot of the other team.

Mo nodded. His cheeks were still bulging with lollies and now Davey noticed his pockets were bulging too. There was no way he'd be able to say boo, let alone bother anyone, with those in his mouth.

Sunil quickly set the rest of his field and they all moved to their positions.

'Just pick up your phone and make that call . . .'

As Tay took up her spot behind the batting wicket and Ivy went to stand at first slip, the two girls continued to sing that awful B4U

song. But when at last Davey reached his place at deep cover, he could no longer hear them. He let out a sigh. *Phew*!

Batfish Beach's opening batters wandered out to take their places. Sunil bowled first, starting with a fast good-length ball outside off stump. The batter seemed unsure whether to move forward or back and in the end let it go through to Tay, who caught it effortlessly.

Sunil's second ball seemed to have the same effect: the batter looked fidgety, unsure, and when he tried to make a shot he missed.

By the middle of the second over, the opening batter was out.

When the next Batfish fronted up at the crease, she too seemed unable to find a rhythm. Sunil adjusted his field, ordering everyone in closer – except Davey and Mo – to put further pressure on the Batfish batters.

Soon a second batter was out, for a total of only fourteen runs. And then a third, caught in slips by Ivy Mundine for six.

Out at deep cover, Davey couldn't really see why things were going so badly for the Batfish. Usually, they were strong in the batting department, probably more so than their bowling. But not today.

In the end, the Batfish middle order crumbled like a cupcake and, with just two batters left, they'd scored a measly thirty-two runs.

As their number ten batter came to the crease, Sunil ordered everyone closer. 'Warner!' he called. 'Your turn to bowl!'

Davey raised his eyebrows. He didn't always get a bowl in real matches, but he liked to keep his hand in if he could.

He crossed the field towards the bowler's wicket. As he drew closer, he became aware of the sound of Tay's voice.

'*You're my one, my only bab-by-y-y-y.*'
Clearly she hadn't stopped for the entire time the Batfish had been batting.

Sunil tossed him the ball.

Davey glanced across at Mo, who was now standing at square leg. The great galoot was still sucking on lollies. *His dentist will love him*, Davey thought.

Davey paced out his run-up and marked the spot. He could still hear Tay singing, but for some reason, when he was bowling, it didn't bother him.

He ran in and bowled a leg-spinner. The batter tried to block it and missed. Tay caught it and in a trice the ball was back with Davey.

This time, Davey put more topspin on the ball, causing it to drop quickly and bounce high. The batter misjudged it, moving forward to drive, but hitting it in the air into the covers. Sunil was there to catch it.

'Out!'

The batter trudged off. There was one Batfish left.

'Keep going, Warner!' Sunil gave him the thumbs-up.

'If you care, if you care at all . . .'

Tay was half-humming, half-singing as she
once more got into position behind the wicket.
It wasn't particularly loud or annoying,
Davey realised now, *unless you happened to
be batting!* Still, he felt sorry for the Batfish
team's last batter.

Davey ran over to Tay. 'Stop singing!' he
whispered in her ear.

Tay looked at him in surprise. 'Oh sure!
Sorry!'

Davey zipped back to the bowler's end
and walked to his mark. He turned and
eyed the Batfish batter. Behind the wicket,
Tay was silent.

Davey ran in and bowled a googly. The
batter thought it was spinning to the off side.

He played at it, but the ball had already turned in the other direction, inside the bat, and it hit the wicket. The bails tumbled.

The Batfish were all out for thirty-two.

CHAPTER 14

THE SANDHILL FLATS SINGERS

'Three cheers for everyone!' Ms Maro threw her arms wide, her face beaming. 'Hip hip hooray!' everyone shouted as enthusiastically as they could. Only Mo was silent, still sucking on a Whopper Chomp.

'Mo, I think you've had enough of those lollies,' Ms Maro said, patting him on the back. 'They're bad for your teeth.'

Mo gulped and swallowed. He looked a little green around the gills. Davey guessed that eighty Whopper Chomps in one afternoon would do that to you.

'Still, you've been quiet as a mouse, haven't you?' Ms Maro flashed Mo a lovely smile.

Davey glanced at Sunil. Ms Maro really *was* cleverer than she let on.

Sunil made as if to wipe his brow. Davey grimaced at his friend in agreement. He still couldn't believe they'd won. Not after everything that had gone wrong.

The team formed two straggly lines and followed Ms Maro back across the park towards school.

As they crossed Flatter Drive, Davey heard the school bell sound. 'So, what happened to McNab, I wonder,' he said.

'Ask him.'

Davey looked up. Sure enough, there was Kevin, wearing dress pants and a red satin shirt.

'How'd you go?' Kevin called as they approached.

'We won, no thanks to you, McNab,' Sunil barked. 'What happened?'

'Spider thing didn't work – at all! Dunno why. Mum just rolled her eyes, grabbed me

by my collar and frog-marched me to the bus stop. It was weird. So I had to dance instead. Sorry.'

He held up the Vegemite jar. 'Here's your spider, Warner, safe and sound.'

Davey took the jar and peered into it. The spider was still playing dead. 'Think I might let him out here. Mum doesn't want him at home.' Davey bent down, unscrewed the lid and shook out the jar. As soon as the spider hit the ground, it scuttled off into the grass.

Ms Maro clapped her hands. 'Now, grab your bags from your classroom and then off you go and have a lovely weekend. You deserve it, guys!'

Davey and his friends set off across the quadrangle towards 6M's room.

Kevin went with them. 'So how did Clouter go?' he said quietly.

'I took care of him.' Tay was just behind them, walking with her new best friend, Ivy.

Sunil and Davey turned to stare at her. 'You?'

'Mo told me he was going to annoy the Batfish and lose us the match. So I gave him all the Whopper Chomps that you gave me, Sunil.' Tay smiled. 'That shut him up.'

Davey nodded. 'Sure did.' He narrowed his eyes. 'But I thought you liked Mo . . .'

'Nah, not really. Shania was right. He's a bit, well, thick.'

'Sure is,' Ivy said. 'For one thing, he hates cricket.'

Tay put her hand in her shorts pocket. 'Here, I saved the last one for you, Davey,' she said, pulling out a Whopper Chomp and handing it to him. 'For getting you into trouble. It should have been me polishing the bowls and sorting the paperclips. Sorry.' She flashed him a wide smile.

Davey shrugged. 'It's okay. Wasn't your fault. Mr Mudge is just a total . . .'

'Mudge!' they all yelled at once.

'Yes?' Mudge had appeared out of nowhere. 'What are you lot doing on school grounds? It's home time. Scoot!' The teacher's ears were already turning magenta.

Without saying anything, everyone ran to the classroom and grabbed their bags.

'Bye, guys!' Tay and Ivy waved before wandering off, arm in arm, singing. *'You're my one, my only, b-a-a-b-b-b-y-y-y!'*

'How could anyone like that song?' Davey frowned. 'And what do they see in that band? Four guys in stupid clothes singing stupid songs in stupid voices. Why do girls like that stuff?'

Sunil grimaced. 'No idea.'

'Nah, me neither,' George said, shrugging. 'It's weird.'

'Totally weird,' Kevin agreed.

They turned and headed for the bike racks. Davey heard a familiar bark. Max was tearing across the playground to meet them.

'War-*ner*!!!' It was Mudge. 'What's that dog doing on school grounds?!!'

'So, why do you reckon the Batfish batting order collapsed like that?' Davey looked across at his best friend. They were lying on the grass out the front, sucking on an ice-block and intermittently throwing balls for Max to chase.

'Gotta thank Tay for that, I think.' Sunil smiled.

Davey took a big bite out of his ice-block and sucked and crunched on it thoughtfully. 'Yeah, well, she's a good wicket-keeper,' he said. 'She's at least as good as Dylan – probably better.'

'She is, but that's not why we won.' Sunil eyed Davey. 'You know how you hate her singing when you're batting? Well, you're not alone. Those Batfish couldn't concentrate.'

'Ah!' Davey had suspected as much. 'So why didn't the umpire tell her to stop?'

''Cause he couldn't really hear her from the other end. It's only annoying if you're batting.'

Max dropped the ball by Davey's hand. It was covered in dog slobber. 'Eeewww!' He picked it up and threw it as far as he could. 'At least Mo couldn't annoy the Batfish,' he said as Max ran off after the ball. 'He was too busy sucking on lollies.'

Davey looked at Sunil. 'And anyway, it's okay to sing, isn't it?'

'Course it is! Especially if you're good at it.'

'Yeah, that's what I thought.' Davey slurped his ice-block loudly. 'And Tay's good at it. She should go on that TV show – *Total Talent Time*.'

'She should,' Sunil said, doing an even louder slurp. 'And I really like that B4U song she sings. It's great.'

'Sure is! I've *always* liked it.' Davey grinned.

'*Just pick up your phone and make that call!*' they sang together in their loudest, most chipmunky voices.

Max looked out from the bushes and howled.

'See? Even Max can sing, the melodious mutt!'

Max howled again. 'Aaahhhooo!'

'Keep it down!' Davey and Sunil shouted.

Hit For Six

DAVID WARNER

with J.S. BLACK, Illustrated by JULES FABER

SIMON & SCHUSTER
AUSTRALIA
A CBS COMPANY

**DEDICATED TO
THE MEMORY OF
PHILLIP HUGHES**

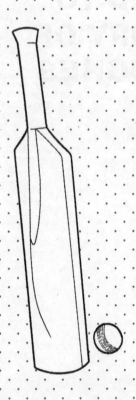

CONTENTS

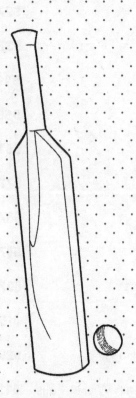

CHAPTER 1
THE BET

'Come on, show me what you've got!' Davey
Warner teased George Pepi, tapping his bat
impatiently at the crease.

George pounded down the rough run-up at
Flatter Park and let fly his fastest delivery.

Davey watched the ball leave George's hand and danced down the pitch to meet it. He swung hard into the ball and . . .

Kaboom!

Davey smacked the ball high into the mid-wicket outfield. He watched with glee as his dog Max let out a yelp in protest. The fox terrier had been fielding at silly mid-off and was surprised at the direction Davey had hit the ball.

'Fooled you, Max!'

It wasn't easy to get one over on Max, who took off at full pelt after the ball. The foxy loved cricket just as much as Davey and his mates.

This was lucky, because playing cricket was all they ever wanted to do. The boys often enjoyed having a hit at Flatter Park on Sundays. It was close to Davey, George and Sunil's homes and Benny's shop was opposite, which was handy for snack breaks.

Max clamped his sharp teeth down on the leather while performing a perfect mid-air 180-degree spin.

'I've had enough of bowling!' George complained, flexing his hand. Davey had been hitting him all over Flatter Park and his hand was getting cramped.

'Music to my ears,' said Sunil Deep, who went to the bowler's end. He much preferred bowling to keeping wicket.

Davey tapped his bat at the crease and waited. He wanted to practise hitting against Sunil's fast bowling. Davey had been feeling really good about his batting lately.

He'd been working really hard with his special bat Kaboom and it felt as if he'd just stepped up to a new level.

With a triumphant air, Max trotted back to Sunil and deposited the gooey ball at his feet. He whined expectantly.

'You're a machine, Max,' chuckled Sunil and gave the dog a scratch behind the ears.

'Here comes trouble,' murmured George.

Chief pest Mo Clouter and his equally annoying sidekicks, Nero and Tony, were walking out to the wicket.

'Just ignore them and they might go away.' Davey was impatient to play. 'Come on, Deep.'

'Why's Clouter dragging a suitcase around with him?' Sunil wondered aloud.

'Maybe he's moving away?' Davey suggested. They could always hope.

Max jumped up and ran towards Mo and sniffed at the suitcase eagerly.

'Has to be food,' said Davey. 'Max! Get back here!'

'I'm starving.' George clutched at his stomach.

'You're always starving,' Davey pointed out.

'Are you our new tea lady?' Sunil asked Mo.

Mo set the suitcase down at the end of the pitch. 'Laugh at me and you'll be sorry!'

'Why's that?' Davey gave up hope of having a hit anytime soon.

Mo gestured proudly to the suitcase. 'Because I have in my possession Benny's shop's entire stock of . . .' Mo unzipped the lid of the case to reveal . . .

'Whopper Chomps!' exclaimed George and Davey in unison.

The suitcase was indeed chock-a-block with packets of the chewy vampire teeth lolly that Davey and Sunil loved.

'You didn't steal them, did you?' asked Sunil suspiciously.

'I used up all my birthday money to buy them!' Mo stared lovingly at the brightly coloured lollies.

'What are you waiting for?' Davey said impatiently. 'Sharing is caring.'

Mo shook his head and crossed his arms on his chest.

'This is a new business venture. You're welcome to some of my stock, but it'll cost you.'

George narrowed his eyes at the unwelcome news. 'How much?'

'$3.50 a bag!' declared Mo.

'Get out of town!' Davey was disgusted. 'You're charging fifty cents more than Benny does!'

'I'm not a charity!' Mo shrugged and explained his scheme. 'A man has to earn a living. It's called supply and demand. Benny won't have more stock for weeks, so in the meantime I'm the only supplier in the market.'

Davey rolled his eyes.

George checked his pockets for loose change. 'How much have you got, Davey? I've got $2.00.'

Davey grimaced. 'I'm broke. What about mate's rates?' he asked Mo.

Mo zipped up his case with a flourish. 'Last time I checked, we weren't mates.'

The bully had a point.

'There's a group of kids playing down by the swings. They could be *real* customers. Time is money . . .'

Mo turned to go.

'Hang on a minute,' said Davey. 'You can't get away with this!'

'I think he just did,' muttered George.
His stomach let out a loud growl.

'It's nothing personal, Shorty. No, hang on,
it *is* personal.' Mo cracked up laughing before
heading off towards the playground, dragging
his case behind him. He turned back and
grinned. 'These are all mine . . . unless you're
interested in having a bet.'

'I'm all ears,' said Davey.

'You've got the game against Shimmer Bay
coming up in two weeks . . .'

'Yeah? So what?'

'If you hit six sixes, then I'll give you *all* my
Whopper Chomps.'

'Six sixes?' George exclaimed. 'That's . . .
like . . . impossible!'

'And if I don't hit six sixes?' Davey asked.

'You have to call me "My Lord and Master" for the rest for the season. You have to carry my footy kit, do my chores. Basically, you'll be my slave.'

'Don't do it, Davey,' Sunil warned.

Davey ignored Sunil. His eyes were fixed on Mo. He'd had enough of the big chump.

'It's a deal.' The words were out of Davey's mouth before he realised he'd said them.

'We each have witnesses, right?'

The others nodded.

Mo held out one of his enormous paws to shake Davey's hand.

'It's a bet!' said Davey as he firmly gripped Mo's hand.

'See you, suckers!' Mo laughed slightly hysterically before taking off with his suitcase.

'You must *really* like Whopper Chomps!' George shook his head at Davey in disbelief.

Davey was up for the challenge. He was looking forward to spending every waking minute of the next two weeks practising his batting so he could bring Mo Clouter down a peg or two. It was way overdue.

CHAPTER 2

MASCOT MADNESS

Monday mornings at Sandhill Primary
began with school assembly out in the
quadrangle. Davey was usually late and this
morning was no exception.

'Ssh!' Davey held a finger to his lips
and slunk in to a place next to his friend

Kevin McNab. He was hoping his teacher Mr Mudge wouldn't notice. Mudge hated students being late. He hated it almost as much as he hated cricket.

'What's this I hear about a bet?' Kevin asked.

Mudge's radar was in fine form. His head spun around at lightning speed at the sound of Kevin's voice. His ears glowed menacingly like hot coals on an open fire.

'No talking!' Mudge hissed at Kevin. He shot Davey a frown for good measure, before turning back to gaze with a look of reverence at their principal, Mrs Trundle.

Trundle had a lot to say, as always. She rattled on about cake stalls, fundraisers, and the upcoming art show and then – just when it seemed she was wrapping things up – she announced a list of merit award winners.

Davey switched off. His name wouldn't be called out. It would be the same students who always won merit awards. Sunil and Bella Ferosi would be among them.

'Sunil Deep,' Mrs Trundle said brightly as she scanned the crowd for Sunil. He stood up and gave her one of his most winning dimpled smiles.

'If I hit six sixes, maybe I'll win a merit award,' Davey whispered to Kevin.

The crowd clapped wearily as Sunil accepted his piece of paper.

'Anything's possible,' Kevin whispered back.

'P-lease,' hissed a voice from behind Davey. Davey didn't need to turn around to know who the voice belonged to. Bella Ferosi.

She knew a lot about winning merit awards and was easily the best student in the class.

'You need *A*s, not *D*s, to win a merit award.' Bella always spoke slowly when speaking to Davey, as if she were speaking to a toddler. It was more than a little annoying.

'You know what, Bella?' whispered Davey.

Bella leaned in closer to hear what he had to say.

'I bet you that I win a merit award by the end of term.'

Kevin's eyes grew wide.

Bella waited for the punchline, but it didn't come. 'Oh, you're not joking?' She narrowed her eyes at Davey. 'That's a bet you're sure to lose.'

'Then you have nothing to lose by accepting the bet,' Davey smiled.

'And if by some freak chance you do win an award?' Bella asked.

'Then you have to dress up as the Sandhill Sluggers' mascot for our final game.'

A small worry line formed on Bella's perfect brow.

'Not the . . . *slug*?' Bella could hardly bring herself to say the word.

Nobody in their right minds ever wanted to wear the Sluggers' mascot costume. And for very good reason.

It was a dark grey–green slug colour with two brown slug antennae sticking dismally out the top. The slug dance was

like the moon walk – no arms, just legs shuffling, dragging the slug's tail.

To make things worse, your face could be seen while wearing the costume. There was nowhere to hide.

'You're serious?' Bella seemed to warm to Davey's idea thinking, perhaps, that there was no way she could lose, because Mr Mudge would *never* give Davey an award.

'And if – make that *when* – you don't win an award, you'll join the All Stars cheer squad for our netball final,' Bella said with an evil grin.

'You mean, in a girl's netball uniform?' Davey asked.

'Uh huh,' Bella nodded, 'pink skirt, pink singlet, pink socks and pink shoes, and you

have to cheer the girls with the pompoms doing *all* the cheers.'

The cheers were ridiculous pop songs sung in soprano with lots of shrieking, giggling and girly hysteria. Something in Davey just snapped. If he was going to bring Mo down, he might as well do the same with Bella. Her opinion of herself was way too high.

'This is not a good idea, Davey,' Kevin warned.

'It's a bet,' said Davey and he shook Bella's outstretched hand.

She smiled politely before withdrawing her hand and wiping the palm on her tunic.

About a century later, assembly ended and they made their way to the classroom.

Mudge called for everyone to settle.

'Just a reminder that tomorrow is our exciting PE excursion to Penguin Palace RSL and Bowling Club and I expect you to be on your best behaviour,' their teacher explained, with something close to enthusiasm.

Mudge even looked less exhausted than usual as he spoke at length about his favourite sport, lawn bowls.

'It will be a long day out in the sun and it's a physically demanding sport . . .'

Davey caught George's eye. Mudge didn't know the meaning of physically demanding and rolling a ball down a small flat green certainly didn't cut it.

'You'll need sunscreen, a hat, sports kit and don't be late for the bus. We leave at 8 a.m. sharp.' The bright vermilion of Mudge's ears highlighted the importance of his words.

Despite the fact that they were in for the world's most boring class excursion, Davey was looking forward to a day out of the classroom.

Surely it couldn't be all that bad?

Bella Ferosi's hand shot up.

'Yes, Bella?' Mudge asked, pleased that someone was showing an interest.

'Sir, will this excursion be assessed?' She shot Davey a smug look.

Mudge grinned. 'I'm so glad you asked, because that was my next announcement.'

Davey's stomach sank with a lurch. It landed somewhere around his knees.

Mudge was grinning from ear to ear like a deranged Cheshire cat. 'Your big assignment for the end of term will be an essay on lawn bowls.'

Davey groaned.

'*Warner*,' Mudge erupted. He went from cold to hot so quickly that the veins in his ears throbbed dangerously. 'You had better be well behaved tomorrow or there will be con-se-quences!'

Davey heard a snigger from Mo.

'Now, as preparation for tomorrow, we will spend the rest of the day studying the history of lawn bowls. If you'll turn your attention to . . .'

And the rest of the day proved to be as mind-numbing as Davey had thought it would be.

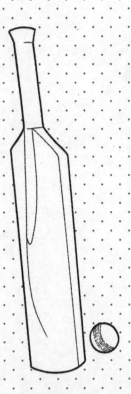

CHAPTER 3

ALARM BELLS

The end-of-day school bell rang out loud and clear.

'The bus leaves at 8 a.m. SHARP!' Mudge yelled as 6M shot out of the classroom as if their lives depended on it.

'I thought he'd never stop,' groaned Kevin.

Davey's head was so full of lawn bowls facts *he* felt old and crotchety.

'I can't believe you've bet your brains and your brawn,' joked George when they were getting their bikes from the bike racks near the school entrance.

'Bella could do with a little healthy competition,' Davey said.

Sunil stifled a laugh.

Davey shot his friend a look which said *Don't you start*. 'I can get a merit award if I set my mind to it.'

'And pigs can fly!' Sunil cracked up.

'Watch it,' Davey said.

'Ooh!' Sunil pretended to be scared. 'Let's see you put that attitude into your batting practice, because you're going to need it!'

'Race you to Little Park,' yelled Davey, taking off in front of the others on his pushie.

'Not if I get there first!' Kevin took off after Davey.

When they got to Little Park, the friends ditched their bikes and got down to business. Davey batted, Sunil bowled, Kevin took his place as wicket-keeper and George was fielder.

While Mudge had been droning on, Davey had spent the day planning his training regime for the next two weeks. He needed to practise his strokeplay, especially hooking, pulling and driving; *then* he wanted to hit sixes.

'Sunil, bowl me some long hops,' Davey asked.

Sunil slyly pitched the ball right up in the blockhole and Davey struggled to get the ball away at all, never mind hitting it for a six.

'Come on! None of this defensive stuff . . . I want to go big!'

Sunil got down to bowling him some long hops and Davey practised his big hits. He focused on following through with his shots. The ball repeatedly soared out of the park.

Sunil nodded at him. 'Better, though the bowlers you'll be facing are faster than me. You're going to need a few magic tricks.'

Davey soon realised what Sunil meant. His arms and shoulders quickly grew tired after slogging the ball over and over again.

Finally he had to admit defeat and call
it a night. His shoulders were aching like
nothing else.

After dinner, Davey brushed his teeth but even
the effort of moving the brush up and down
was agony.

'You need to toughen up,' he told the
mirror.

Davey flexed his biceps and checked out his
reflection. He grimaced at his sore muscles.

Davey's older brother, Steve, appeared in
the doorway.

'Hey, Rambo,' Steve teased.

Davey grunted and continued brushing.

'I heard something about a bet with Mo. You reckon you're going to hit six sixes at the game against Josh Jarrett?' Steve asked.

Josh Jarrett was Shimmer Bay's captain and cricket's all-round Mr Perfect. Josh and Davey enjoyed a long-running grudge match.

As far as Davey was concerned, losing to Josh was something he couldn't bear to think about.

'Mmm.' Davey rinsed his mouth with mouthwash.

'I'll be there to cheer you on,' said Steve, clapping Davey on the back.

Whoosh! Davey spat out the mouthwash.

'You think I have a shot at winning?' He was stunned to think his brother had faith in him.

 524

'Mate, you've got Buckley's.' Steve chuckled and grabbed his own toothbrush.

Davey groaned. He didn't have the energy to argue. He dragged himself down the hall and flopped into bed.

As soon as Davey opened his eyes, he knew something was wrong. The room was too bright, the house too quiet. He rolled over in bed and looked at his digital clock.

8 a.m.!!!

The digits flashed at him urgently. Davey's brain was sparked into life with a jolt. He'd been so tired the night before he'd forgotten to set his alarm.

'AAAHHH!' Davey sat upright. He felt real and immediate terror. The bus for their excursion was leaving at 8 a.m.!

Mudge would be mad as a maggot.

Max bounded into the room and jumped onto Davey's bed. He looked happy and carefree.

'Move, dog!'

Davey pushed Max out of the way and leapt out of bed. If he hurried, he might still make it!

CHAPTER 4
THE HITCHHIKER

Davey sprinted down Eel Avenue towards
school. His backpack bumped jerkily,
digging into his spine. Despite his stiff
shoulder muscles, he pumped his arms like
pistons to sprint as fast as he could.

'You can do this,' he told himself between gasps for breath.

Just as Davey reached the corner of the street and could see the school grounds, he heard the familiar sound of claws on cement running alongside him.

'Max,' he hissed, 'go home now!'

Max refused to do anything of the sort. Davey lunged at the dog. The foxie bounded past Davey's outstretched arms and raced across the road towards school.

'Ugh! You mongrel!' Davey yelled.

He sprinted around the corner just in time to see a large bus pull out from the kerb.

'No! Wait!'

Davey sprinted as fast as he could after the bus but it accelerated as it pulled into the traffic. He felt as if his lungs might explode and reluctantly slowed to a halt. He bent over to catch his breath. Max jumped up and licked his face.

'I have two words for you,' muttered Davey, pushing the pesky dog away. 'Dog pound.'

For once Max looked contrite. He sat down abruptly and smiled with a butter-wouldn't-melt expression on his face.

'You don't fool me, mutt.' Davey tried not to panic and thought about his options. There was nothing to be gained by going to school now. He'd end up doing chores for Mrs Trundle all day.

In fact, the more Davey thought about it the better he felt. Suddenly he had an entire day free to practise hitting sixes!

'You're brilliant, Max!'

Max wagged his tail. He'd apparently known this all along.

'Warrr-*ner*!' A familiar drawl interrupted Davey's dreams of the perfect way to spend a day.

'Eh?' Davey turned to see Mr Mudge staring at him from the other side of the street.

'Why aren't you on the bus?' asked Mudge, whose ears were beginning to turn a magnificent magenta.

'I'm sorry, Sir, I slept in and missed it,' called Davey. He glared down at Max. *This is all your fault.*

'Lucky for you I'm taking my own car, so I can give you a lift!' Mudge replied cheerily.

Davey had never seen his teacher look so . . . *happy.* He noticed Mudge's old pale blue Morris Minor parked outside the front of the school. The teacher unlocked the car and opened the front passenger door.

'Hop in. I'll just grab some paperwork from the office and we can go.'

Davey exhaled a long sigh. He couldn't play cricket, but at least he wouldn't get into trouble with his mum or Mudge.

The only problem was he needed to get rid of Max before Mudge saw him. Mudge hated Max. The dog was banned from school grounds, but that had never stopped him – a fact which caused Mudge much displeasure.

'Go home, Max!' Davey commanded and pointed in the direction of Eel Avenue. He didn't have time to take the dog there.

Max cocked his head and ignored Davey completely. Then, quick as a flash, Max leapt into Mudge's car and curled up on the passenger seat.

'No way, Max!'

Davey had just about had enough of the dog's hijinks. 'Mudge hates you even more than he hates me, and that's a lot.'

Max seemed unmoved by Davey's revelation.

Then Davey caught a glimpse of Mudge's mustard-coloured skivvy and panicked.

'Quick, Max!' He unzipped his backpack and beckoned for the pesky pooch to get inside it. Max loved curling up in small spaces, so he trotted into the backpack and settled into a tight ball with his head sticking out of the opening.

'Keep quiet, or else!' Davey warned him. 'Just remember – dog pound.'

'Seat belt on please, Warner.' Mudge took his seat and started the engine.

Davey hugged his backpack to his chest so that Max's face was hidden. It wriggled slightly.

'Come on, boy. Throw your bag in the back, there's plenty of room,' Mudge commanded.

'Ah, no, it's fine here, thanks.' Davey gingerly placed the backpack at his feet and buckled his seat belt.

Within moments, the sound of Max's gentle snores drifted up from the floor.

Davey coughed loudly. 'Do you have any music, Sir?' he asked.

'As a matter of fact, the wireless is tuned to Classic FM,' Mudge smiled at Davey. He reached over and soon the car was flooded with the sound of classical music.

Davey thought it sounded like cats fighting, but at least it drowned out Max's snoring.

The drive to Penguin Palace Bowling Club would only take about ten minutes in a normal car with a normal driver. Mudge,

however, took slow driving to a new level.
He never allowed the speedometer to go above
40 kilometres an hour.

It was going to be a very long trip.

CHAPTER 5
THE CURVE BALL

Mudge parked in front of the Penguin Palace Bowling Club.

'Hurry up and get carrying, Warner,' Mudge instructed. 'I have some of my own bowling ball collection that needs to come inside.' He opened the boot of the

car to reveal boxes upon boxes of lawn
bowls.

'All of these,' Mudge clicked his fingers
at Warner. 'Be careful, they're heavy,'
he added before disappearing inside
the club.

Davey was on his third trip carrying boxes
when the bus finally pulled up.

'Oi, Teacher's Pet!' Mo squashed his huge
gob against the bus window and made faces
at Davey.

Bella Ferosi jumped up to see who Mo was
talking to. Teacher's Pet was *her* nickname!
She seemed perturbed to see Davey working
as Mudge's personal helper.

'Getting a merit award by sucking up
to the teacher doesn't count!' she whispered

threateningly to Davey as she sashayed
past and grabbed a box of lawn bowls
to carry.

Once everyone was off the bus and inside
the club, Mudge called for quiet.

'This is my club. You had all better be
squeaky clean and your best selves today or
you will live to regret it. Am I clear?'

'Crystal, Sir,' the class droned in unison.

'Hear that, Max?' Davey whispered to his
bag. The bag huffed.

Mudge divided the class into four groups.
Davey and George were on the same team,
Sunil and Kevin in another. Mo and Bella
were in another still.

Sunil picked up a bowling ball from the box. 'Weird shape,' he commented. 'Just like your head, Mo!'

George cracked up. Mo glared at him and grabbed a bowl from the box. He drew back his arm and sent it hurtling dangerously down the green. The ball veered sharply to the right and careered off into the gutter.

'Oi, my ball is broken!' Mo shouted.

'Keep your voice down, Mr Clouter! There are other people trying to play here.' Mudge smiled apologetically at the other members playing on a rink further down the green.

'As Mr Clouter here has just shown us,' Mudge explained to the group through clenched teeth, 'the bowls are not round.'

He held up a bowl to demonstrate.

 540

'That's just dumb,' Mo huffed.

'The aim of the game is to get your black bowling ball as close to the white jack as possible,' continued Mudge.

'Now, this isn't as easy as it looks. It takes precision, skill and lots of practice.'

Davey shot Sunil a look. *Come on . . . !* Mudge was talking about a tiny square piece of lawn made up of perfectly manicured grass. It was nothing like a cricket pitch and certainly didn't require any muscle.

As Mudge explained more about the game, he looked as close to contented as Davey had ever seen him.

'The bowls are weighted to one side so they will curve towards the place you want to hit. How much it turns depends on how fast you roll it and where you aim it. Rather than straight, you are aiming to send the bowl in an arc shape.'

Mudge selected a bowl and held it out to Bella. 'Miss Ferosi, why don't you have a try?'

With a firm flick of her ponytail, Bella accepted the challenge. She rolled her bowl down the green in a perfect arc and it came to a rest just beside the target.

Mudge's pale face flushed with pleasure and he burst into a spontaneous round of applause. 'Someone in this class was paying attention! Thank you, Bella!'

Bella shot Davey a 'beat that' look.

A flash of colour and movement caught Davey's eye.

'Uh oh,' he sucked in his breath.

Davey's backpack was heading inside the club towards the bar. He'd forgotten all about Max! While Mudge droned on, Davey excused himself, saying he needed to go to the toilet.

'Max!' Davey hastily grabbed the backpack and carried it with him to the toilets. He unzipped the bag and gave the dog a drink of water.

'You need to lie low for a little while longer,' he told the dog.

Max bristled.

'Come on,' coaxed Davey.

Max gave a low growl.

'I'll make it worth your while, I promise,' Davey pleaded. 'Lots of doggie treats!'

Finally Max stalked slowly into the backpack and lay down with a huff. Davey placed the backpack carefully alongside the other bags. When he joined the group again, Mudge was demonstrating how to bowl using the shape of the ball to its best advantage. 6M clapped on cue as he sent a ball rolling at a snail's pace down the green.

Then Mudge announced he would give each student an individual lesson. It would take about two thousand years to get through them all.

'Wake me up when it's my turn,' whispered Kevin. He closed his eyes and rested his head against a pole.

'Warner!' Mudge barked.

Davey jumped to attention. 'Yes, Sir!'

'Let's see what the mighty cricketer can do!' Mudge licked his lips.

Davey selected a bowl and felt its weight. He judged the distance to the jack and tried to picture the arc the ball would travel along. He drew a line in his mind's eye.

As the bowl left Davey's hand, he saw a white blur flash through the corner of his eye.

No!

Max was tearing across the green after the ball.

'Max!'

It was all too horrible. Max ignored Davey's ball and plucked the jack from the green and held it expertly between his teeth.

'WARNER!' Mudge roared. 'Get that dog off the green!' He sounded close to hysterical and his ears had turned a bright fire-engine red.

Mo's laugh broke out through the chaos and Davey turned to see the bully lying on the ground in stitches. He writhed around, pointing and laughing.

Max had gone crazy – now that he was free he was tearing around in circles, barking in a frenzy. But the real problem was that, every time he changed direction, he tore up big tufts of green turf which flew into the air like confetti.

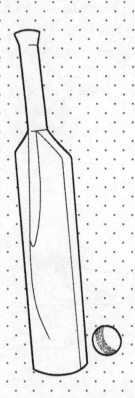

CHAPTER 6
MAD MAX

Max was like a dog possessed as he zigged and zagged across the square green.

A crowd had gathered from inside the club room. Horrified *oohs* and *ahs* soon drowned out Mo's maniacal laughter.

'Max, you monster!' Davey tried to grab Max, but the foxie was having none of it. He dodged and weaved like a football pro. At one point he stopped and, for a second, Davey thought he had a chance to grab him.

But the dog began to furiously dig a hole in the green. Then he dropped the small white ball neatly into it.

'Max!'

Then, to top it off, Max cocked his back leg and peed into the hole.

It brought everyone to a standstill. There was a horrified silence which was broken by the sound of Mo laughing again.

Davey buried his head in his hands.

The crowd burst into stunned but slightly admiring applause at the audacity of the small dog.

'WARNER!' Mudge erupted. He was positively apoplectic. His ears were almost black. 'Get that dog off the green NOW!'

Sunil, Kevin, George and Davey closed in on Max. The mad mutt lay down and rolled over, completely tuckered out. Sunil picked him up and tucked him firmly under one arm. He gave Davey a look of sympathy.

Max had done a lot of damage in a very short amount of time. Now the green was less a green colour and more a brown patchwork pattern. Aside from the clumps of dirt, Max had dug two decent-sized holes.

Mudge walked around the green muttering to himself. Then he went unusually quiet.

 551

The excursion was cancelled.

Davey was doomed.

'There, there,' crooned Bella with delight, patting him on the back.

Mo was still laughing.

Back at school, Davey had to suffer through Mo and his cronies' endless sniggering, Bella's superior smiles and general loathing from the rest of the class. He was officially an outcast, as the whole of 6M blamed him for ruining a day out and having to be back at school before lunchtime.

'I want a word with you, Warner,' Mudge drawled as the bell finally rang for the end of day.

It was the first time the teacher had spoken to him since they left the bowls club.

Good luck, Sunil mouthed to Davey as he and the others filed out of class.

'As punishment for your dog's appalling behaviour today' – Mudge spoke so quietly that Davey strained to hear him – 'you will volunteer at the bowling club every day for the next two weeks.'

Davey opened his mouth to protest, but thought better of it. He would still have time to practise cricket before school.

'By every day, I mean before school and after school,' Mudge continued.

Davey whimpered. He thought about his two bets and how impossible it was going to be to win either.

 553

'I have already spoken to your mother,' Mudge continued, looking at his desk. He was so angry he couldn't even look at Davey. 'Personally, I don't want you anywhere near my club, but it was their decision. You will start work tomorrow morning.'

'Mr Mudge . . .' Davey began.

'Are we understood?' Mudge brought his fist down hard on his desk with a thump.

Davey jumped.

'Yes, Sir!'

Davey left the classroom and made his way over to the nets for cricket practice. The team had already begun having a hit, but their coach Benny was nowhere to be seen.

'What's the punishment?' George asked.

'I've got to spend the next two weeks at the bowls club.'

Sunil's eyes grew round. 'Mate, you have no chance of winning the bet. Call it off with Mo now.'

'No!' Davey said stubbornly. 'I don't give up on a bet.'

'Suit yourself,' Sunil answered.

Just then, Benny arrived. 'Gather round, lads,' he called, trying to get his breath back.

The team gathered around their coach.

'Our next game is a bye and then we have the big one with Shimmer Bay.' Benny stuck a porky finger into one nostril and had a good dig.

'We have no chance. I just want you guys to do your best. It's all we can hope for.'

'Do you have a strategy, coach?' asked George.

Benny stared off into the distance. 'Not as such. Just watch out for that Josh Jarrett. He's a player to watch. Going places he is.'

Davey kicked at the dirt with his foot.

Benny glanced at his watch. 'Is that the time? Got to get home for tea.' He waddled off in the direction of his shop.

Sunil rolled his eyes at Benny's departure and the team went back to their cricket practice while it was still light enough to play.

'What are you going to write for your lawn bowls assignment?' Practice was over and Sunil was packing up his kit.

'I thought I'd write about the bias,' said Kevin.

George shrugged. 'I liked the team spirit.'

'Warner?' Sunil asked.

Davey shook his head, 'Dunno, Deep. I really haven't given it much thought.'

'You should,' Sunil replied, 'if you want to beat Bella and win a merit award. It's our last major assessment for the term.'

'Thanks for the advice . . .' Davey muttered. He grabbed his Kaboom bat and marched off home.

Davey was about to spend all his spare time at a bowling club. The last thing he wanted to do was think about Mudge, or anything to do with lawn bowls, for that matter.

CHAPTER 7

AGAINST THE BIAS

Davey had made sure to set his alarm for an early start the next morning. It would take at least half an hour to ride to Penguin Palace Bowling Club and they wanted him to put in a full hour of work before school.

When he wheeled his bike inside the club gate, Davey shuddered at the sight that met his eyes. The green looked as if a herd of elephants had stampeded across it. He had a flashback to the sight of Max peeing in the hole. The horror!

'You must be David!' a tanned, grey-haired man wearing faded green overalls greeted him.

'Everyone calls me Davey,' Davey replied, 'except Mr Mudge, of course.'

The man straightened up from weeding the flowerbed and smiled. 'And what does Vernon, I mean Mr Mudge, call you?'

'WARRR-*NER*!' Davey replied, giving his best impersonation of Mudge.

The old man chuckled.

'Nice to meet you, Davey. I'm Trevor and I'm the greenkeeper here.'

They shook hands. Trevor glanced at Davey's backpack.

'Is there a dog in your bag, by any chance?'

'Uh, no,' Davey squirmed, 'not this time, anyway.'

'Made quite a mess, he did. Some of the members were very upset,' Trevor continued.

Davey shoved his hands in his pockets and stared at the ground. 'I – I – I'm really sorry,' he stuttered.

'Thanks Davey.' Trevor lowered his voice. 'This lot need stirring up every now and then, if you ask me.'

Davey looked up. He wasn't sure, but he thought he saw a twinkle in the old man's eye.

'Do you like lawn bowls?' Trevor asked.

'Yeah?' Davey sounded about as convincing as Benny did when asked if the Sluggers had a chance.

Trevor nodded. 'It's not for everyone. Grab some gloves and get to work weeding with me. I'm sure you're not too pleased to be here, but I'm grateful for some help. My back's not what it used to be.'

Davey thought Trevor looked really fit and strong for his age. 'What about the green?' he asked.

'We'll get to that. Plenty of time.'

Davey picked up a pair of gardening gloves and got to work. He hadn't even noticed the gardens when he was here for the excursion. The bowling green was surrounded by garden beds filled with flowers and small shrubs.

Weeding was boring, but after a while Davey kind of zoned out and didn't mind it so much. Trevor whistled as he worked and it was nice to be outside in the fresh air. It was better than being in detention or picking up rubbish at school.

'You'll probably want to get off to school soon,' Trevor said when they had finished the final garden bed.

Davey stretched. His shoulders and back ached. He'd never realised gardening was such physical work. 'See you this afternoon, then,' he said and picked up his bag.

He was wheeling his bike out when he noticed a familiar face.

It was Josh Jarrett. He was walking to school with a few other boys from Shimmer Bay Primary.

Davey thought about turning around, but it was too late. Josh had seen him.

'Warner?' Josh called. 'Given up on cricket, then?'

'You wish,' Davey retorted.

'Maybe it's time for you to retire. Lawn bowls might be more your speed!' Josh erupted in fits of laughter.

Trevor and Davey shared a look.

'I heard about your little bet!' Josh continued. 'Warner here reckons he can hit six sixes during our game,' he explained to his mates.

Everyone burst out laughing.

'That little squirt?' asked one of Josh's friends.

Josh nodded and pointed at Davey.

Davey said nothing. Trevor looked intrigued.

'Six sixes in a game against me . . . ?' Josh slapped his knee. 'You're dreaming!'

Davey met Josh's gaze coolly. He was becoming immune to others laughing at him. 'See you at the game, Josh.'

Josh walked off laughing.

'Let me guess: he's an excellent cricket player, even if he is a bit arrogant,' Trevor said.

'His team is current number one and he also plays for the rep side.'

'Yep, I hate him already.'

Trevor pulled his cap further down his head and got back to work. 'See you this arvo, then.'

Davey took that as a signal to head off to school.

He thought about what Josh had said as he rode to school. He now had very little time to practise big-hitting and Josh would make sure everyone found out about the bet.

Davey was going to be the laughing stock of the whole town.

CHAPTER 8
SLEEP ON IT

For the rest of the day, Davey couldn't stop
yawning. This gave Mudge a great deal of
satisfaction.

'Tired from doing some honest work
for once, Warner?' the teacher asked with
a smirk.

Davey thought he had a nerve – Mudge was always exhausted.

'That's the trouble with your generation – no work ethic.' This inspired Mudge to launch into a monologue about how the values of 'young people these days' were on the decline.

Davey blocked Mudge out. He was thinking about how to get some cricket training into his already packed week.

At least Mudge seemed to have calmed down about the Max incident now Davey was serving his penance.

Mo, on the other hand, wouldn't leave Davey alone. 'Not much time for batting practice with all the gardening you'll be doing!' he whispered to Davey while Mudge's back was turned.

'That was low,' Davey hissed back. 'How can I practise my hitting if I'm stuck at the bowls club every waking minute?'

Mo leaned in so close that Davey could smell his breath. *Phee-ew!*

'Not my problem, Warner.'

'Can I help you two?' Davey looked up to see Mudge standing over them both.

'No thank you, Sir,' said Mo innocently. 'David and I were just discussing the lawn bowls assignment, Sir.'

This placated Mudge, who went back to droning on about wayward youth and how unemployable they all were.

Mo winked at Davey. 'No Whopper Chomps for you, Warner.'

Davey didn't reply. As much as he hated to admit it, Mo had him. He had him right where he wanted him.

Sunil, Kevin and George were still playing cricket at Little Park when Davey rode his bike there that evening. He'd come straight from the bowls club. There were still a few minutes left of daylight and Davey had been itching to practise a new batting trick he'd thought about all day.

'Guys, the legendary MS Dhoni had a brilliant helicopter hit that always got him sixes,' he announced, picking up Sunil's bat to demonstrate. The famous Indian player would hit the ball upwards and then follow through with his bat twirling above his shoulders in a circular motion. When played well, it looked like a helicopter rotor.

Sunil guffawed. 'This I've got to see.'

'I know, I need to practise it, but maybe I could use it to hit a six off a good-length ball.' Davey stifled a yawn. 'Borrow your bat?' he asked Sunil.

'Sure, I'll bowl.'

Davey grabbed his helmet and fastened the straps. This was a trick that required head protection.

Sunil walked back up to his mark and turned to face Davey. Kevin got into position as wicket-keeper and George fielded at first slip.

Sunil went easy on Davey and the first ball was slow compared to what he'd have to face against Shimmer Bay. He swung hard at the ball and tried to spin around in a circular movement after the bat. He spun so fast he nearly fell over.

'You need strong arms and a really fast bat speed for the helicopter shot to work,' Sunil pointed out.

Davey knew his mate was right.

'Bowl on a good length,' Davey instructed, 'and let me see what I can do.'

Sunil bowled the next one short of a length and as it passed Davey at waist height, he swung at the ball but only succeeded in sending it straight up into the air.

The following ball was well up, but Davey swung too late and only managed to pop the ball straight back to Sunil.

'Not as easy as it looks on YouTube. It's hard to time it right,' Davey lamented.

But he kept practising and after several more tries he succeeded in hitting a beauty right out of the park.

It was almost dark. 'Better go finish my essay for Mudge,' said Sunil.

'Don't tell me that's due tomorrow?' Davey asked with a groan.

'Okay, I won't!'

Davey gave him a look. 'Is it?'

Sunil nodded.

Davey sighed. He was utterly spent. 'Better get to it, then,' he muttered and headed across the road to his house.

Davey's mum had kept his dinner warm.
He realised he was starving and bolted down
his favourite meal of sausages and mash.

'Thanks, Mum!' Davey gave her a quick kiss
on the cheek and headed to his room.

He opened his schoolbook and stared
at the blank page. The lines began to blur.
His muscles were sore, his stomach was full.
It had been a long day.

Within minutes, his head had fallen onto
the desk. Davey was fast asleep.

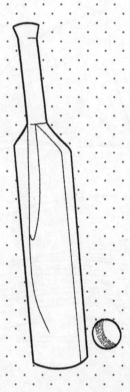

CHAPTER 9
CAUGHT OUT

Davey spent the next morning before school helping Trevor at the bowling club. They laid new turf to try and patch the holes Max had made.

'Not bad,' said Trevor when he saw the job Davey had done. The green was already

beginning to look more green than brown. 'I'll water it while you're at school.

'*School*?' Davey checked his watch. He was going to be late!

Davey rode like crazy and made it to school just as class was about to begin. He slipped into the room and quietly took his seat. He felt a deep burn in his thighs from pedalling so fast. His muscles were going to stiffen up sitting all day.

Bella caught his eye and held up a piece of paper and mouthed the words 'A-plus' at him. Davey remembered with a jolt: *The essay!* He hadn't done it.

'Oh no!' Davey hoped like crazy that Mudge would forget to ask for their essays until after lunch. Maybe then he could write his during the lunch break.

'Shall I collect the essays?' Bella Ferosi asked Mudge, with a triumphant look at Davey.

Davey groaned. So much for that.

Mudge clapped his hands together eagerly. 'Thank you, Bella. Lovely to see someone with drive and initiative.'

Bella was out of her chair in less time than it took to say Teacher's Pet.

Davey shot Sunil a panicked look. The friends had to sit in opposite corners of the room so they couldn't talk about cricket. Mudge loathed cricket almost as much as he loathed students who didn't hand in their assignments.

Sunil understood immediately. He shot his hand up.

'Yes, Sunil?' Mudge asked.

Sunil flashed his dimple. 'I was wondering if you'd mind repeating yesterday's equations, Sir? I didn't quite understand.'

'Not like you, Mr Deep.' Mudge began writing out an equation on the whiteboard.

Davey gave Sunil the thumbs up. Maybe the distraction technique would work.

With his back still turned, Mudge asked Bella, 'Miss Ferosi, how are you going with those assignments?'

Or maybe not. Davey felt doomed.

Bella was making her way around the room slowly. She ticked each name off a list

with a determined flourish as she collected each paper.

'Nearly done, Mr Mudge.' Bella moved a little faster.

'Take a seat, Miss Ferosi, I'll collect the rest myself.'

Bella handed Mudge the pile of essays. Mudge scanned the checklist.

'Just two to go. Mr Clouter and Mr Warner.' Mudge held out his hand impatiently to Davey and Mo.

Mo handed over two sheets of paper held together by a silver paperclip. Mudge added it to his pile.

'Warner?' Mudge clicked his fingers impatiently. 'Come on, we don't have all day.'

Davey gulped. 'It's like this, Sir . . .'

Mudge raised an eyebrow. 'You're not going to tell us your dog ate your homework, are you, Warner?'

There were a few sniggers from around the room.

'Although, knowing your mutt, I wouldn't put it past him.'

Davey squirmed.

'With all the extra work at the bowling club, I . . .'

'*Yes?*' Mudge leaned over him.

'With all the extra work at the bowling club, I . . .'

'Spit it out, Warner!'

'I fell asleep, Sir,' Davey finished lamely.

Mudge rocked back and forth on his heels. 'A shining example to the rest of the class about the pitfalls of leaving everything to the last minute.'

'Sorry, Sir,' Davey added.

'You will be!' Mudge brightened up slightly. He obviously lived for moments like this. 'You're on lunchtime detention for the next two weeks. And I want that essay finished by Monday.'

'But with the work I'm doing at the bowling club, I won't have any time,' Davey argued.

'I *own* you for the next two weeks!' Mudge roared. *'Am I clear?!'*

Davey knew it was pointless to argue. 'Crystal, Sir.' He slumped lower in his seat.

Mo nudged him sharply with his elbow. 'Lord and Master,' he guffawed.

Bella, who sat on the other side of Davey, leaned in close to him. 'I hope you've been practising your cheers,' she smiled brightly.

Bella was right. In no time, Davey would be wearing a pink skirt and chanting netball songs. He was sunk.

Now Davey had absolutely no time to practise his big-hitting. And there was no way in the world he was going to win a merit award. He imagined wearing pink and cheering the netball team while Mo snacked on Whopper Chomps and Davey was his personal slave.

He couldn't bear to think about it.

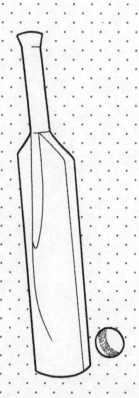

CHAPTER 10

ROLLING, ROLLING, ROLLING

At the bowling club after school, Trevor led Davey to the storage shed. Inside was a huge, ancient-looking metal roller.

'You've got to be kidding.'

The roller looked more like a museum relic than a functioning piece of machinery.

'You know you can get ride-on rollers these days like they use on cricket pitches?' Davey asked.

'Is that so?' Trevor said with a wink. 'Well, we've got nothing that fancy here.'

He lifted the handle and began to pull. 'Stop your gawping and come and help me,' he said, straining against the weight. 'This thing weighs a ton.'

Davey grabbed the other side of the handle and helped Trevor pull the roller out onto the green. It was slow going. Like a slug.

'We've done the best we can with the grass. Just a matter of time before it grows back,'

Trevor explained. 'But now we need a level playing surface.'

'You want *me* to push this thing?' Davey asked.

Trevor looked around. 'I don't see anyone else lining up for the job, and I'll be mowing the professional green.'

He nodded his head for Davey to get to work.

Davey inspected the roller. *Yikes.*

'Okay. I can do this,' he told himself. He leaned down, picked up the steel handle and leaned all of his weight into it as he pushed. The roller barely moved.

Davey tried again. He grunted with the effort. The roller moved a few centimetres.

'Yes!'

There was a smattering of applause. 'That'll toughen you up,' said an old man who was watching him from the side of the green.

Another old codger gave Davey the thumbs up.

'Young people today don't know about physical work.'

The other oldie agreed and they fell into a whinge-fest about how things were so much harder back in their day.

'I'll show you wrinklies,' Davey muttered to himself. He braced his arms, keeping them slightly bent but strong, and leaned forward with all his might. The roller moved forward with a jolt and this time Davey was able to keep the momentum going.

After what felt like four hours but was only ten minutes, Davey had rolled three metres of green. He stopped for a break.

The old codgers were still watching and one of them motioned for him to join them.

'Not bad for a young punk,' said one.

'Thanks,' Davey said flatly. His shoulders were already beginning to ache.

'You know,' said the other codger, 'Trevor can roll this whole green in the time it took you to do that measly effort.'

Measly effort? That was a bit harsh.

'Has Trevor always worked here?' Davey asked.

'Old Trev? Nah, he used to work in cricket.'

Davey's ears pricked up. 'Cricket?'

'He looked after all the big pitches – The Gabba, SCG, you name it. The man knows his cricket. He has a few stories to tell, does Trev.'

The members fell back into their own conversation and Davey realised he'd been dismissed. If Trevor could do it, then Davey Warner could. He resolved to finish rolling the green.

He went back to the roller and gave it his all.

Davey was thoroughly exhausted by the time he got home. He'd had a major upper body workout at the bowls club, and a lower body workout on his pushie riding the ten kilometres there and back twice a day.

All he wanted to do was eat and go to bed as soon as he got home.

Davey's mum had other ideas. 'David Warner, get in here right now. You've got some explaining to do.'

Uh oh. Davey froze in the kitchen doorway, but he was too tired to make a run for it.

He found his mum pacing the lounge room. That was a bad sign.

She pointed to the couch. 'Sit.'

Davey sat down.

'I just don't understand,' his mum began. 'First there's this business with the bowls club and you and Max running riot. Now, Mr Mudge says you don't even bother handing in your assignments.'

Davey groaned. 'It wasn't like that, Mum.'

'If you put the same amount of effort into your schoolwork as you do into cricket, you'd be top of your class!'

'Sorry, Mum. I did try but I fell asleep.'

'Aha!' His mum pounced. 'Fell asleep because you're so tired from playing cricket every minute of the day. Well, that's all stopping right now.'

'Er, what's stopping?'

'Cricket. No more until you write the essay. I know you have a big game coming up, but you won't be playing in it until the work is done.'

'But Mum!' Davey wanted to explain about the bet and hitting six sixes, but he was worried it would make her even angrier.

He was starting to think she might be right.

His mum gave him some left-over corned beef and vegetables for dinner. He could barely lift the fork to his lips because he was so tired.

'Bed!' said his mum, once he'd eaten.

'Bed,' sighed Davey as he sank into his mattress.

He stretched out his aching shoulders and fell into a deep and dreamless sleep.

CHAPTER 11

BEHIND THE SCENES

Davey was finished.

He looked back over his work from the last few days and felt a deep sense of pride. His arm muscles felt it too. He had worked all weekend and the social players' bowling green was now perfectly rolled.

Trevor clapped him on the back. 'I think you deserve a break.'

Inside the club, Trevor bought Davey a club lunch and a lemonade. They sat together at a window table and looked out over the green.

'I heard a rumour that you used to look after cricket pitches,' said Davey before gulping down some lemonade.

Trevor chuckled. 'For most of my life.'

'Did you ever play?' Davey asked.

'As a kid I did, but later I liked watching more. I've seen lots of the big games. But I like the behind-the-scenes stuff better.'

The bartender brought their meals over and there was silence while they both tucked into hamburgers and chips. Davey realised he was ravenous.

'So how's Mr Mudge going, or should I call him Mudge?'

Davey rolled his eyes and finished chewing a mouthful of chips.

'He's on my case. I've got to hand in an essay tomorrow about lawn bowls and I don't know where to begin.'

'Why don't you write about what you've learned working here?'

'Gardening?'

'How to prepare a pitch for play. It's the same with cricket. As a player, you have to learn how to read the pitch. Someone has meticulously prepared that piece of grass

to be level and the moisture of the soil has to be just right or cracks appear. What happens if a crack appears and you bowl or hit a ball onto it?'

Davey thought about the question. 'The ball could go in a direction different from where you expect it to.'

Trevor nodded. 'Exactly! So, in order to read a pitch or a bowling green properly, you need to learn how to maintain it. In bowls as in cricket, the condition of the grass affects the path and speed of the ball.'

Trevor had a point. Davey knew about the pitch affecting his game, but he'd always been rubbish at turning it to his advantage.

'If you can read a pitch correctly, then you might just be one step ahead of your mate Josh Jarrett.'

Davey realised for the first time that there might just *be* something to the game of lawn bowls.

'Want me to show you how to play bowls properly?'

Davey nodded.

Once they had finished their meal, Trevor collected a bag from the storage shed and took it with him out to the green. He unzipped it and pulled out two beautifully polished bowls. He handed one to Davey.

'You already know the bowl is shaped so that it will roll in a curved direction. Now, I know this green very well and I know that it's slightly uneven – it sinks a little lower in the left corner – so I'll keep that in mind when I play. Also, some greens are fast and some are slow. We have quite a slow green.'

They had a game and some of the members even gathered around to give tips. Davey realised that bowls was a very social sport and before too long he was enjoying himself.

'You can have a rest day tomorrow and then it's back to more rolling,' said Trevor, when it was time to head home.

'But it's all done,' protested Davey, pointing to the social green they'd been playing on.

'You're ready for the big league son,' Trevor chuckled, pointing to the professional players' green next to the one they had worked on.

Davey groaned.

That night, Davey tidied his room. He never tidied his room. Yet he found himself packing toys away, putting dirty clothes in the wash basket, and neatly lining up his cricket trophies so they faced out just so.

Once his room was spotless, he began to vacuum the lounge room floor.

Davey's mum eyed him suspiciously. 'As much as I love the fact that you're helping around the house,' she said, 'I think it's time to start your essay.'

'The dirty dishes are still in the sink!' protested Davey.

'Now!' His mother frogmarched him to his room and sat him down at his desk.

She was right. If he didn't hand his essay in the next day, he wouldn't be allowed to practise his hitting, let alone play in the match.

Max wandered into the room and jumped up onto Davey's bed.

'Hey, mutt,' said Davey.

Max circled three times and then lay down with a huff.

Davey yawned. He looked down at his blank piece of paper. Wow. He'd been sitting there for ten minutes and hadn't written a word.

Trouble is, maybe Bella's right, he thought. *Maybe I'm just not very academic. Mr Mudge doesn't seem to think I am.*

Davey really felt like a Whopper Chomp.
Or something sugary to eat. Or anything to
eat. Or a drink. He got up to go to the kitchen.

'Not so fast!' Davey's mum was waiting in
the hall outside his bedroom.

'Are you stalking me?' Davey asked.

'Essay,' she said firmly.

'I'm hungry,' Davey complained.

Davey's mum smiled knowingly. 'I'll bring
you a snack. And a drink. Now go!'

Davey sat back down at his desk and
knew that this was it. No more excuses.
He thought about Trevor and the care and
attention that went into looking after the
bowling green.

Davey wrote at the top of the page, 'Behind the Scenes by David Warner'.

Then he began to write.

CHAPTER 12

BAD GUYS AND UNDERDOGS

The next morning, Davey met up with Sunil, Kevin and George at C playing field before school.

'Hey, stranger,' called Kevin. Then he hit a ball straight into George's outstretched hands at silly mid-off.

'Howzat?' cried George.

'Aw!' Kevin walked.

Davey and Kaboom took their place at the crease. It felt good to be back. Sunil obliged by bowling him a few so he could practise his new shot.

'Woah!' Davey realised just how rusty he was when he spun around so fast he fell over.

'You'll be calling me Lord and Master before too long,' snorted Mo, who seemed to have appeared magically out of thin air.

Mo was flanked by Nero and Tony, who apparently both found Mo's comment to be utterly hilarious.

Davey knew it was better to ignore Mo in the hope he would vanish, but this morning he took the bait.

'You don't know what you're talking about, Clouter,' he said. 'You know nothing about cricket.'

'I know you've done zero cricket practise for the last week,' the big galah screeched. 'The Whopper Chomps are mine, *all mine!*'

'Don't be too sure,' said Davey. 'I'm the underdog and everyone loves the underdog.'

'The chances of you hitting six sixes are zero,' the big hunk of wood guffawed before lumbering off.

Davey managed to get a few hits in before the bell rang.

The four friends made their way to the classroom. Most of 6M had already taken their seats, but Mudge was nowhere to be seen.

Bella Ferosi gave her ponytail a distracted flick when she saw Davey take his seat.

'End of term is getting closer, David,' she said and held up her pocketbook calendar. 'Not much time left to get a merit award.'

Bella flashed Davey her perfectly even white teeth in a well-practised, yet insincere, smile.

'So should I measure you up for a costume?' she continued. 'Pink will really suit your skin tone.'

'Just like slug colour will really suit yours,' Davey shot back.

They locked eyes.

Davey waggled two fingers above his head like slug antennae waving in the breeze.

'Don't mess with me, Warner,' Bella replied, her voice as cold as steel. 'There's only room in this class for one teacher's pet.'

Davey mimed the slug dance and hummed the Sluggers' song.

Finally Mr Mudge arrived.

'Good morning, 6M.' He dabbed at the back of his neck with a stained handkerchief. 'We have computer studies first up this morning, so grab your workbooks and we'll head over to the lab.'

Davey shot up his hand.

'What is it, Warner?' Mudge snapped, with more than a hint of impatience.

'I have my lawn bowls essay for you, Sir.'

'Ah, yes!' Mudge looked so surprised he almost fell over. 'Bring it over.'

Davey threaded his way past chairs and desks and held out the essay to Mudge.

'Just put it on my desk,' Mudge said dismissively. 'I'll get to it later.'

'Yes, Sir.' Davey placed the essay on Mudge's desk.

Mudge peered at the title page and sniffed as if the essay somehow offended him.

'I imagine it won't take me long to read if it's your usual standard.'

Davey ignored Bella's look of triumph on the way back to his desk.

The next few days passed in a blur for Davey. He worked with Trevor before and after school. He kept his head down in class and tried to be a model student. He helped Mudge polish endless supplies of lawn bowls during his lunch break. And when he could he practised his six-hitting.

All too soon, it was the night before the big game against Shimmer Bay.

Davey struggled to get to sleep. After a few hours of tossing and turning, he turned on his light and sat up in bed. Max gave a snort of protest but went back to sleep.

Davey looked up at the faded poster of his hero, Ricky Ponting, which hung above his bed. Ricky was smiling and, despite the fangs that Sunil had added, it gave Davey confidence to imagine he was talking to the real Ricky.

Davey imagined Ricky was standing at the crease – he stared straight ahead, concentrating on the ball coming his way.

'Everyone's out to get me, Ricky,' Davey told his hero. 'I've set myself up for the impossible. And now all the people who want me to fail are going to get what they want.'

'It's not over until the last wicket falls.'

'What?' Davey could have sworn that Ricky had spoken, but the face in the poster just stared back at him.

Davey turned the phrase over and over in his mind and eventually fell asleep.

CHAPTER 13
AGAINST THE ODDS

Nothing could have prepared Davey for the size of the crowd gathered at the cricket ground.

'Holy moly,' he murmured.

Word of the bet had spread like wildfire throughout the school. Kids from kindy

through to Year Six were keen to see if Davey Warner could indeed hit six sixes. Nobody wanted to see him become Mo Clouter's personal slave.

Davey noticed that most of 6M were there. He could easily pick out Mo's big head. He noticed that Bella was also in the crowd.

'You're going down, Shorty,' growled Mo when he saw Davey. 'Prepare to lose.'

Davey gave Mo a friendly wave and scanned the rest of the crowd.

Rob, the selector for the rep side, was there. He was always on the lookout for new talent. Seeing Rob made Davey's stomach lurch with nerves.

'Davey Warner!' Rob nodded and waved his little notebook.

Talk about pressure.

But the biggest surprise was that Benny was there on time before the start of a big game.

'So miracles do happen!' said Sunil. He and Davey shared a look.

'Oi, Sluggers!'

Benny called the team together for a pre-game pep talk. He shook his head sadly at the fate that awaited them.

'It takes real courage to lose well,' Benny began, and he adjusted his belt over his protruding belly. 'The fact that you guys have got this far should be reward enough.'

For once, Benny was right. There was a general muttering of agreement from the

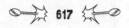

team. After all, everyone knew that Shimmer Bay were virtually impossible to beat.

'I even heard a joke that Davey is going to hit six sixes!' Benny grabbed his generous stomach and let out a huge belly laugh. 'Funniest thing I've ever heard, hey Warner?'

Davey cleared his throat. 'It's true, Coach. What's more, we're going to win. We're going to beat Josh Jarrett and Shimmer Bay.'

Benny laughed so hard that big tears rolled down his chubby cheeks. 'You boys, you keep me young.' He wiped the tears away. 'I need to go and eat something before the game.' He belched loudly and wandered off towards the canteen.

Sunil gathered the team in closer.

'Davey's right,' said Sunil in his captain's voice.

It was hard not to get carried away by Sunil's sunny disposition and sense of authority. 'We've got this far because we're good. We're going to take this team down and claim our rightful spot at number one!'

The team let out a cheer.

The Sluggers won the toss and opted to bat first. Because it was such a big game, it was going to be played over two innings. They had their work cut out for them.

As Shimmer Bay made their way out onto the field, Josh Jarrett tipped his cap curtly to Davey.

'Hey Warner, I see your bowling cronies are here to support you!' He held up his

thumb and forefinger in the shape of an
L for 'loser'.

Davey didn't know what Josh was talking
about until he saw a small group gathered
under a tree. Trevor and a few of the other
guys from the bowls club were sipping tea
from plastic mugs.

'Bowl me over!' Davey chuckled to himself.
Just about everyone he knew was gathered
together to watch this game.

Then Davey saw something that nearly did
bowl him over.

Mudge was standing with Trevor.

It made *no* sense. Mudge hated cricket!
He *detested* cricket. Davey didn't have time
to figure out Mudge's agenda, because it was
time to play.

The Sluggers got off to a shaky start, losing their two openers early in quick succession.

It was Davey's turn to bat. This was his big moment.

As he walked out, Sunil gave him a big thumbs up.

'Go, Davey!' called his family.

Despite the crowd watching his every move, Davey did his best to block everything out. It was him and Kaboom and the ball. He tightened his grip and tapped Kaboom against the crease.

'Let's see what you've got, Warner,' snarled Troy, Shimmer Bay's fast bowler.

Davey felt quietly confident and started hitting the ball very sweetly. He kept his head down and allowed himself to warm up.

Before too long, he had reached thirty-five, with two well-struck sixes under his belt.

'Boo!' Mo jeered.

'You can do it, Davey!' Trevor yelled. The bowlers let out a whoop.

Davey grinned and then, in a rush of over-confidence, he decided to try the helicopter shot.

He hit the ball high on the bat and succeeded only in looping it to backward square leg, where the fielder took an easy catch.

He was out.

George got his head down and, with some help from Tay Tui, they pushed the score on to 128 all out.

When Shimmer Bay came in, they started steadily, with Josh batting well. However, Sunil was at his deadly best. He dismissed three of their top order and continued to trouble all the batsmen.

When Josh was on forty-two and the Shimmers were three down for eighty, Sunil enticed Josh to play at one outside the off stump. It left him just enough to catch the edge of his bat and wicket-keeper Tay took a straightforward catch.

The remaining Shimmer batsmen managed a few more runs, but eventually they were all out for 116, with Sunil taking seven wickets.

In the Sluggers' second innings, they again lost their opening batsmen early. Davey was well aware of the responsibility he carried and played within himself while he accumulated runs.

With the score on two wickets for sixty-two, the Shimmers' fast bowler tried a short of a length delivery at Davey. He stepped inside the line and smacked it straight over the square leg fence.

Clearly annoyed, Troy bowled another, even faster, ball but Davey repeated the dose.

He had now hit four sixes.

'Way to go, Davey!' his dad shouted.

'Two to go,' Davey said to himself.

The Sluggers lost another wicket, but Davey bided his time, waiting for the right ball. At three for ninety-four, with Davey now on forty-six, their off-spinner tossed one up. Davey took two paces down the pitch and hit it straight over his head and over the sightscreen. Five sixes!

The crowd erupted as, with the shot, he brought up the team's hundred and his own half-century. Davey clocked Mo looking worried.

Davey realised that his arms and shoulders had held up. He wasn't as tired as he thought he would be.

Trevor . . . ! Davey thought. He realised that all the work he'd done at the bowling club had given him the upper body strength he needed.

Several overs later, the Sluggers had a good lead and Davey was in the sixties.

It's now or never, Davey thought, with the last over about to be bowled.

Davey tried the helicopter shot on a well-pitched ball from their medium-pacer. He swung himself almost off his feet and the

ball left the bat like a bullet from a gun. Davey heard the crowd gasp as the ball soared over wide mid-on.

He'd done it! Six sixes!

The crowd went ballistic. Davey Warner had hit six sixes and won the bet.

Sunil ran to Davey from the non-striker's end and nearly knocked him over with a hug.

'That was incredible!'

Davey felt completely stunned.

'Where's Clouter?' Davey asked Sunil. 'I feel like a Whopper Chomp or twenty.'

The friends scanned the crowd to see Mo taking off from the grounds as fast as his legs could carry him.

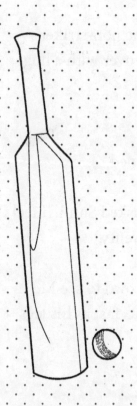

CHAPTER 14

THUGS, SLUGS AND BEAR HUGS

At the break between innings, Davey found himself surrounded by friends and well-wishers. People were lining up to congratulate him.

'Knew you could do it, kid brother.' Steve ruffled Davey's hair.

Trevor shook Davey's hand enthusiastically.

'Good for you!' Benny enveloped Davey in a bear hug. 'I was backing you all the way, son.'

'Warner?'

A familiar voice caused Davey to turn. 'Sir?'

Mudge looked so grim that Davey knew for sure he was a goner. It made sense now. Mudge couldn't wait until school to tell him he'd failed his assignment.

'I read your essay on preparing the green in order to play a game of lawn bowls.'

Davey noticed Bella Ferosi sidling up next to them. *Her ears must be flapping*, he thought. He'd be decked out in pink in no time.

'Yes, Sir?'

Mudge suddenly broke into a smile.

'I am pleased to say that you surprised me, Warner. The depth of research that you went into was impressive. And I have to say it gave me a new appreciation for the game of cricket.'

Davey's jaw dropped.

'I have given you an A.'

Bella scowled.

Davey's jaw dropped even further.

'What's more, I've sent your name to Mrs Trundle for the next round of merit awards. I think you'd better be on time to assembly on Monday.'

'Thank you, Sir,' Davey managed to say.

Was Davey's hearing working? Did Mudge just give him an A for his essay *and* a merit award?

He must have, because Bella was now trying to sneak away.

'Not so fast, Ferosi, you're not going anywhere!' He grabbed Bella's arm. 'We have a beautiful slug costume with your name on it.'

Bella shot Davey a withering look, but she went with Sunil and George.

Davey wolfed down an orange and then it was time to head out to field. After all, they still had a game to win.

The Sluggers weren't out of the woods.

Thanks to Davey's innings, they were leading by 147 runs, but the Shimmers were still very much in the game.

Josh was in great form. He'd taken Davey hitting six sixes badly and wasn't about to let go of the game. He smashed another four to the fence.

Despite excellent bowling from Sunil, the Shimmers were scoring quickly. The Sluggers' morale was dropping steadily and Sunil gathered the team together for a quick pep talk.

'We can do this!' he said cheerily in his captain's voice. 'After all, we have a secret weapon!'

'First I've heard of it!' Ivy said drily.

'What's our secret weapon?' asked Tay.

'That!' Sunil pointed to an odd-looking slug-coloured creature standing on the sidelines. Two limp antennae drooped from the top of its head.

The Sluggers' slug mascot had arrived.

'What *is* that thing?' cried Josh in horror.

'The slug!' cried the team.

A huge cheer rang out from the Sluggers supporters. Despite burning cheeks and looking as if she might die of embarrassment, Bella Ferosi began to perform the slug dance. To her credit, she gave it all she had.

'Sluggers! Sluggers!' chanted the crowd.

Though wickets fell at regular intervals, Josh continued to play very well. He was like a man possessed. He handled all the Sluggers bowlers, including Sunil, with ease.

With the score at seven wickets down for 144 and Josh at the crease, things were looking grim for the Sluggers.

Sunil brought himself back on for one last effort.

Josh edged the first ball on the ground through the slips cordon and ran a single: seven for 145.

Next ball, with a mighty effort, Sunil produced an unplayable delivery that pitched on leg stump and seamed away to knock the batsman's off stump out of the ground: eight for 145.

The Shimmers' number ten came in looking distinctly nervous. Sunil bounded in and pitched a full one straight at his toes. He backed away but managed to get his bat up, and the ball looped in the air to point, where Davey took a simple catch.

The score was now nine for 145.

In came the Shimmers' number eleven. Sunil was again in top form. He got the batsman to edge the ball, but even Tay, flinging herself to her right, could not hold the difficult chance.

Josh rushed through for a single to get the strike.

Sunil bowled to Josh as fast as he possibly could, but over-pitched.

Josh slammed the full toss back down the wicket straight at Sunil. He valiantly tried to catch it, but it burst through his hands and hit him on the inside of the kneecap.

'Oohhh!' gasped the crowd.

Sunil went down like a sack of spuds, writhing in pain.

No run was taken and the Sluggers crowded around their captain. He definitely couldn't bowl any more and was helped off the field.

Shimmer Bay needed only two runs to win.

One wicket to fall.

One ball left in the over.

Who was going to bowl it?

'Give it to me,' said Davey. 'I'll bowl.'

He and Josh Jarrett locked eyes.

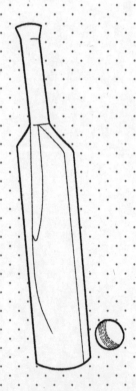

CHAPTER 15

'IT'S NOT OVER UNTIL THE LAST WICKET FALLS'

Davey had noticed when he was batting that at the crease where Josh stood there were one or two cracks in the pitch outside the off stump.

If he could land the ball on one, he might just get it to move around a bit.

'Ha!' Josh smirked as Davey got ready to bowl. 'The lawn bowler! Perfect.'

Josh had no idea just how right he was. Davey was a lawn bowler and a greenkeeper. But he was also a cricketer.

'This one's for Josh,' Davey told the ball.

Davey ran in holding the ball with his fingers on either side of the seam. The ball pitched a little short and Josh stepped back, intending to smack it away on the off side.

But the ball caught the edge of the crack and seamed wickedly back in to Josh. Completely surprised, Josh only succeeded in getting a thin inside edge.

Tay flung herself to her left at full stretch and just managed to glove the ball in her left hand.

Josh Jarrett was out! Tay and Davey had done it between them.

The Sluggers had won by one run.

'YAAAYYY!'

The new number ones on the ladder sprinted around the pitch faster than any slug you've ever seen. Even the slug got into the spirit. Bella was picked up by the crowd and carried around the field. The Sluggers were heroes!

It had been a sensational weekend, but Monday came around as quickly as ever.

As Davey pulled up at the school gate, he noticed Mo and his mates lurking.

'Wondered when you'd show up!' Davey held out his hand for the suitcase. 'Hand it over.'

Then Davey noticed Mo's face.

'You look awful,' Davey said. He wasn't trying to be mean. Mo *did* look awful. He looked green and shiny. He was sweating profusely and his hair hung limply on his head. In fact, he looked more like a slug than Bella had in costume.

'I'm sick,' Mo groaned. 'Something I ate . . .'

Mo looked like he might projectile-vomit any second. Davey took a step back.

'Anyway, my dad said all Clouters hold up their end of the bet, so . . .' Mo handed over to Davey the Whopper Chomps suitcase.

'Thanks, Mo. It takes a big man to admit when he's wrong.'

Mo began to back away slowly.

Davey unzipped the suitcase to reveal . . . nothing. The case was empty.

'Hey!' Davey called to Mo's retreating back.

'Sucker!' Mo turned and jeered. Then he clutched his stomach. 'I think I'm going to throw up . . .' He headed for the toilets at a rapid pace. 'Too many Whopper Chomps . . .'

He couldn't have eaten all twenty packets on his own, could he?

The bell rang.

For once, Davey Warner was on time for assembly.